THE
GREENING

BOOK TWO:
IN THE WAVE

CONSTANCE SPRAGUE

SILVER BEECH PRESS

PART ONE

It began with a touch. A sense of penetration so slight, it registered as a whisper on the wind. But it didn't stop there.

While the planet slowly revolved on its tilting axis, the prickling sensation spread, grew stronger, more insistent. Could it be happening again? *She mused. The problem had risen before, as problems do, vexing Her into such a firestorm of cleansing and renewal that She had anticipated no further nonsense from that quarter.*

Yet there it was, irritating, electrifying and undeniable; someone was sowing Deep Magic on Earth again.

She let out a patient sigh that shook the trees in two continents. Perhaps it would run its course and vanish into the ether. Perhaps the humans would control themselves better this time. Sure. That would happen.

She smiled and the sun blazed down on North America. She closed her eyes and went back to sleep. Perhaps to dream. As She drifted off She thought, when I wake that little prickle had best be gone.

***

In the shadowy depths of the great Cascade forest one giant fir stands out from the rest due to a lingering haze of shimmering energy still pulsing from root to branch. The man who once spent nine months inside the tree is gone, but his ghost remains in the tree's memory; his thoughts and feelings still echo in the tree's fiber and spread through the microbial systems that spiderweb beneath the soil, connecting to other root systems, linking to other forests. Magic of a kind not seen on Earth for years beyond counting soaks into the soil and rises up in the mist to be carried to faraway hills and other branches, there to evaporate and join the clouds, awaiting a ride down on the rain. The threadbare tapestry of possibility is about to be rewoven.

Buckle up, children. It could be a wild ride.

CHAPTER 1

Shiloh pushed open the door with her duffel bag and dropped it on the floor. She looked past the empty front room to the dining area in the back. The old rowhouse had the stale, inert atmosphere of a funeral home.

"Hello?" she called.

She made a quick tour of the downstairs. Josh's computer was gone, but that wasn't unusual.

She headed up the narrow, creaking stairs. A golden light filtered through the leaves outside the upstairs hall window, brushing the wood floors with gleaming warmth. But the house felt oddly cold and lifeless.

"Eva?" Shiloh called, even though by this time she didn't think anyone was home. She turned the knob to her own room and stopped just inside the door, sensing something out of place.

Her glance traveled quickly over the familiar surfaces—her chair, her desk, her bed...

A piece of paper lay on her pillow. She stared at it as if it might be explosive. When she looked closer, her heart stuttered on a tug of recognition. It was a letter she'd seen before. Nearly ten years had passed since she had read it and carefully hidden it in a box at the back of her closet. A wave of nausea hit her as she realized that someone else must have read it, and leaving it out on her pillow wasn't Josh's style.

She sank onto the bed and picked up the letter.

Dear Shiloh,

I know I promised I would leave you alone. But I can't go on like this without knowing if you are all right. You should have told me about the baby. Maybe you were right to leave, but you never gave me a chance. I understand you wanting to be with your family, but that doesn't make it right for you to take our child.

Lyra told me. She told me that you wanted me to be with her.

You know how I feel. I don't understand why you did what you did, but there's still time for us. Let me come to you. I can help you. I want to help you. I would do anything for you.

Please give me a chance. I deserve that much.

Forest

"Oh, shit," Shiloh muttered.

She got up and looked first in Eva's closet. It was hard to tell if anything was missing, but then, Eva had never cared much about clothes. Shiloh turned to the bureau. She yanked open the top drawer. It was mostly empty.

The physical evidence was slender, but the hollow feel of the room was unmistakable.

She pulled out her old cell phone—antique compared to the latest photo-synth models but still functioning—and punched in Josh's number. He picked up on the first ring.

"Hey! You're home early."

"Where is she?"

"Who?"

"Eva. Who else?"

"What do you mean? Isn't she there?"

"If she were, I wouldn't be asking you, would I?"

"Hey, I saw her this morning before she left for school. Maybe she stayed after for something."

"No. She came home. And now she's gone."

"How do you know?"

"Where are you? Can you come home now?"

"Sure, but do you think maybe you're overreacting? She's twelve now. She's more independent."

"I know that. But... just come home, would you?"

"Okay. I'll be there as quick as I can."

Shiloh lay back on the bed. Dizziness enveloped her. Every muscle ached and her eyes burned from lack of sleep. This trip had been harder than most, or maybe she was just getting worn down by it. It wasn't getting easier.

In the first few years, when Eva was a baby, it hadn't seemed so overwhelming. Her trips across country and around the world were short and always successful. The outbreaks of magic were small and easily contained or eradicated. For a while, Shiloh rode high on a wave of confidence fed by a diet of steady victories.

But as Eva grew bigger and became more active, more inquisitive, the challenges Shiloh faced on her job also grew more complex, more time consuming. The containment spell that had locked down the first signs of Deep Magic was less effective at stopping the spread of mutant energy that flared like gas fires through gaps in the containment shield.

This last trip she'd had to face down a whole tribe of radical loonies in Texas who'd been smoking the fireweed and conjuring baby dragons. Shiloh dreaded the day when some fool figured out how to unleash problems too powerful for her.

And there was no one she could turn to for help. Josh, a wiz at all things technical and digital, barely grasped the concept of magical transformation. She'd given up trying to unravel the links between chemistry and magic for him. In her darkest moments she sometimes wished Magda would send reinforcements.

The last thing she needed was to have to worry about a runaway kid. It didn't help that she felt responsible. She'd never felt at ease in the maternal role. It happened. She gave birth. It was awesome. But the dark-eyed child who stared so coolly up at her even while sucking on Shiloh's engorged breast had never seemed all that innocent. Shiloh didn't know if other mothers felt this strange sense of distance from their own children. Once so close, yet always so far away in their own minds.

And now...where would she have gone? *If I'd found that letter I know what I would have done. Gone to find my Dad. Don't wait up.*

But Shiloh had been twenty-three when she left to search for her missing father. Eva was twelve. And the world was a different place. A much different place.

By the time Josh arrived from Capitol Hill, Shiloh had already mapped out an itinerary of places to search. She had no intention of involving the police or the government. There were too many secrets at stake.

She barely glanced at Josh when he came in. He watched her scrolling rapidly through websites listing missing children.

"What's your plan?" he asked.

She didn't take her eyes from the screen. "I'm going to find my kid."

"She's not going to be on those sites."

"I know that."

"So why are you wasting time...?"

"Don't you dare criticize me! You were supposed to be taking care of her. Where were you when she left?"

"I had to go in to the office for an emergency meeting. She's a big girl now. She knows how to take care of herself."

"That wasn't the deal. You were supposed to keep her safe."

Josh clenched his jaw and said nothing. In the twelve years they'd lived together, they had never fought. At first, after Eva was born, when Shiloh seemed almost at peace, Josh had fantasized about the possibility of becoming more than a supportive friend. When she was relaxed and happy, Shiloh charmed him in a way his former fiancé never had. There was something about Shiloh that kept Josh from being able to even look at another woman. And on the rare occasions when Shiloh had shown anger he hadn't been afraid of her. Somehow it made her even more appealing. But this was different. Her anger was directed at him.

"Hey! I'm not to blame for this. I've done everything you've ever asked me to do. And I would have done more..."

Shiloh scowled and hung her head. "Right. Right. It's not your fault. I should have..." She dropped her head in her hands and muttered, "I should have seen this coming."

Josh pulled up a chair and sat next to her. "What makes you so sure she's gone?"

Shiloh pulled the letter out of her back pocket and handed it to him.

He read it in silence. Then he looked at her and said, "I guess you waited too long to tell her."

"How was I supposed to tell her? I'm not that good at lying."

"Maybe you should have told her the truth."

Shiloh snorted. "That's easy for you to say. How much of the truth? Should I have told her about the grafters and the whole 'your grandpa used to live inside a tree' thing? You think she would have believed that?"

"You're her mother. She would have believed you."

"Huh. Maybe. She sure isn't gonna believe me now. Not after reading that."

"Don't sell her short. She's smarter than I was when I was twelve, and I was pretty damn smart. If you could explain the whole story, the way you did to me... I believed you."

"So I guess you're not all that smart." Shiloh shot him a small smile and Josh felt that familiar pull, the longing to be needed by her.

"Well, there's no point in second guessing. We just have to figure out the best way to look for her," he said.

"She's not going to make it easy. And I can't stop doing my job either. The magic's getting stronger—like it's feeding on itself or something. As fast as I stamp it out in one place it's firing up in ten others. I don't know how much longer I can do this alone. I need a team."

"You have me." He tried a winsome smile, but she didn't seem to notice.

"I need you here. You've got to be my anchor." She looked at him then, her gray-green eyes drawing him in.

"Whatever you want," he said.

They put their heads together then and discussed the most likely options Eva would have used to get far away as fast as possible. They ruled out the bike, though she may have started that way. They also ruled out the stagecoach routes. Eva would have known they could track her through that system, primitive as it was. And she couldn't drive yet, as far as Shiloh knew, so even if she'd been able to get her hands on a photo-synth car she wouldn't have been able to operate it. Probably.

Shiloh tried to recall if any of Eva's friends had horses. Eva was always nagging Shiloh to get her a horse of her own. If Eva had "borrowed" a horse from one of her friends, she could be miles away already.

Shiloh closed her eyes and willed herself not to worry. "She'll be fine. She'll be fine. She'll be fine," she whispered to herself.

"Did you say something?" Josh looked at her from the kitchen, where he was throwing together a quick meal and some food for her to carry.

"No. I'm just...tired. A night's sleep would have been sweet."

"Maybe you should rest before you leave. You're not going to find her tonight."

Shiloh shook her head slowly. "I have to go now."

She packed a small bag with her usual magic tools and a few other essentials and left the house as the sun was going down around six. The shorter days and colder temperatures wouldn't help, but maybe they would drive Eva to shelter somewhere. Shiloh trudged off down P Street wishing she had had the foresight to embed a tracking chip in her child. So much for being laid-back and liberal, she thought.

She headed for the vent at the edge of Rock Creek Park, took a deep breath, and slipped through.

CHAPTER 2

Eva Carter had never seen a traffic jam.

By the time she was old enough to say the word 'car' the only ones left operating on Earth were the electric-and-solar-powered hybrids left over from the end of the oil age, back when no one took alternative fuels seriously.

After the Greening, when all the oil and oil products on Earth reverted to their vegetative origins, new methods had to be found, or revived, to supply the world's essentials. Cars, which had once seemed so vital to modern life, fell out of the top ten most critical needs. People scrabbled for food, water, medicine, heat, and clothing. Shoes alone occupied a special niche on the must-have scale. Durability and utility once more trumped style.

Some writers, posting helpless rants on the still-functioning strands of the internet, complained about the beginning of a new Dark Age. Others touted the clean air and water, the relative silence, the return of dark nights with starry skies no longer bleached out by electric glare.

There was no question that it was a quieter world without jets and trucks. But it was a hungrier world—and, in many ways, a more dangerous one. As the government's inability to respond quickly to emergencies became apparent, a new breed of outlaws rose up to claim unguarded territories. Pirates on land and sea preyed upon those who ventured too far away from the cities. People formed militias armed with swords and clubs. Guns were scarce and bullets scarcer.

Activists who embraced the new order urged the populace to recover lost skills—farming, blacksmithing, boat building. Water wheels and millers reappeared. Engineers and mechanics refining the new technology of photo-synth energy salvaged supplies from trash heaps to cobble together gadgets that could run on sunlight. Horse theft was a growth industry.

Eva reined her stolen horse to a stop and pulled out the old paper map she had grabbed on impulse when she left her bike in Mandy's garage. She knew Mandy would figure out that she had stolen the horse as soon as she saw her bike, but Eva had no choice. She had to have a horse, and Mandy was a rich kid. Her parents could buy another.

The map didn't help as much as she'd hoped. She had to get across the Potomac and find Route 66, the only road she knew of that went west. She remembered Josh borrowing an electric car and taking her and her mother out to Virginia once, when she was a little girl. It had taken forever. Eva had no idea how long it would take on horseback. It had cost her the better part of the night just to get to Mandy's house in Bethesda. Since leaving there, she had stayed on something called River Road, an overgrown expanse of cracked pavement that went on for miles. According to the map, it would take her to the Beltway, the big ring of roads surrounding D.C., and from there Eva hoped it would be easy.

She pulled her jacket tighter and stared into the darkness. She was already hungry, but although she'd stuffed a bunch of food in her backpack she didn't want to start eating it. She had brought all the money she could find. But she didn't know how long it would take to get where she was going. In her mind she lightly skipped past that gaping hole in the plan. She'd figure out where she was going once she got far enough away.

A few hours later she had managed to find the Beltway. The sun glinted on the river as she crossed the bridge over the Potomac, and she enjoyed a moment of elation when she saw an old sign that read, "Welcome to Virginia."

A hovercraft suddenly appeared above the tree line and skimmed off toward the city. Eva shuddered anxiously. Her shoulders already ached and her eyes were burning. She wished she could rest for just a little while. But if her mother caught up to her now, would she ever have the courage to leave again?

Maybe her mother had some really good explanation for the letter. Maybe her father had been a terrible man.

Eva closed her eyes for a moment and the words in the letter rose like bile in her mind. A bad man wouldn't have written such a letter. A fresh wave of anger kindled in Eva's chest. She straightened up, shook the reins, and pressed on into Virginia.

***

In the weeks that followed, the golden glow of October faded and the chill of autumn nights began to make Eva wish she'd packed better. She traded her camera for a blanket at a barter post in Kentucky, but it wasn't near enough.

She squinted in the noonday sun sparkling on the Missouri River. The water was muddy from heavy rains the night before, the air still damp and chilly in spite of the sunshine. She pulled her jacket closer around her body. Her long dark hair hung in a heavy braid down her back. The weight of it was like an old friend, but as she considered her options with winter closing in, she knew the smart thing to do would be to cut her ties, and her hair. A few hours later the tail was gone. The remains were pretty ragged—she hadn't brought a pair of scissors and the knife she'd used wasn't a precision tool. Still, it was a start. She headed for the road that led back to the last town she'd passed through. She didn't relish spending any of her limited money on anything but food, but she figured she could afford a bottle of peroxide.

The next day the temperatures fell even lower. A rim of frost glazed the windows of the houses she passed on her way into the next town. Catching sight of her reflection in the window of a small photo-synth shop, she almost didn't recognize herself. As her focus shifted from the surface of the window to what was inside, she noticed a woman staring back at her.

In the two months since she'd left D.C., Eva's only guiding principle had been to keep moving. A moving target was harder to find, she reasoned. She knew her mother would be hunting for her. Maybe the cops too, although, from the things she'd heard from kids on the street back home, the cops had their hands full just keeping a lid on looting and random violence.

She wanted to keep going west. But that would mean crossing the Great Plains in winter. And the Rockies, if she made it that far. She was determined to get to Seattle, one of the only places she had heard her mother mention that was far away. While trying to puzzle out why her mother had never told her about her father being alive, and why he had never tried to see her, she had come up with a theory that it was because he was physically far away. And maybe he didn't know where Shiloh had gone. The letter had been addressed care of Shiloh's parents in North Carolina.

In truth Eva hadn't a clue how to find Forest, but the first step was to avoid being found herself.

On impulse she got down, tied up the horse, and went in the shop.

The woman who had been staring at her through the window continued to stare silently. Eva returned the favor, noting the woman's graying hair, slender frame, and sour expression.

"What do you want?" the woman asked. The store smelled like rust and burning rubber.

"I'm looking for a job," Eva said.

The woman snorted softly. "What can you do?"

"I don't need money. I just need a place to stay for the winter. I can do chores, clean, cook... take care of horses."

"We ain't got any horses." The woman looked Eva up and down. "How old are you?"

"I'm twelve. Almost thirteen."

"Thirteen is trouble. We don't need no more of that."

"I wouldn't be any trouble. I just need a place to stay until spring."

"Where's your people?"

Eva frowned. "My mom's dead." She hesitated, trying to keep her face blank.

"What about your pa?"

"He left. He swore he was gonna find the men that killed her. He left me with a neighbor. But she got sick and now I'm on my own. That's why I'm trying to find my dad."

"Huh." The woman turned away from her and stared toward the back of the shop, from which small pinging noises drifted in the dusty air.

After another quiet moment she said, "I reckon you can stay tonight." With another glance to the back room she added, "We'll see about tomorrow."

Eva gazed around at the clutter. Every manner of once-modern gadgetry appeared to be represented, all of them hot-rodded to function without a conventional source of electricity or any oil-based lubricants. Toasters, hair dryers, radios, lamps, even a few small cookstoves crowded the shelves.

There was no sign of the shop's most coveted offering— the photo-synth cards that turned sunlight into usable energy. Those precious wares would be locked in a safe, though no place was really safe anymore.

Eva sat down on a dusty chair and waited while the woman went about her business, closing up the shop for the day.

The woman glanced out at Eva's horse and said, "That your horse?"

"Yes," Eva replied.

"You don't want to leave it out there. We got no place you can keep a horse."

Eva frowned. "Don't you have a backyard? I could just tie it up for the night."

The woman shook her head. "You can tie it up all you want. No guarantee it'll be there come morning."

Eva weighed this for a moment. If she lost the horse she would just have to get another somehow. "I guess that's a chance I'll have to take."

She went out and led the horse around back of the building. She gave it the last of her feed, covered it with the blanket, and tied it up as best she could.

When she went back inside the woman locked the front door and motioned to Eva, leading her through a narrow hall to a kitchen with a small table and two chairs. The scent of beans cooking made Eva's stomach burn. It had been a while since she'd had a hot meal.

"Sit," the woman said. Then she gave Eva a look and asked, "You got a name?"

"Angela." The woman continued looking at her for a few seconds, as if measuring the probability of that being Eva's real name. These days identity theft wasn't a top concern for most people. They were too busy worrying about more immediate ways of being robbed.

"Well, Angela, why don't you go bring in the other chair."

Dinner was a quiet affair. Walter, the woman's husband, seemed uninterested in Eva's presence. She guessed that she wasn't the first stray to share a meal with them.

Afterwards the woman lit a candle and led Eva upstairs to a chilly, narrow, dingy room outfitted with a cot and a few blankets. As the woman turned to leave Eva said, "Excuse me. What's your name? I mean, what should I call you?"

The woman paused at the door. The candlelight fickered; shadows trembled over her face. After a slight hesitation she said, "My name's all I got left. I'll tell you what it is if you end up sticking around for a while." She turned away again, but added, "We don't have no TV," before she left Eva on her own.

No TV works for me, Eva thought. She didn't want to see her face show up on one of those "Have You Seen This Person?" shows that ran several times a day on the National News Network, the only network still broadcasting regularly.

She lay back on the cot and took a deep breath. She'd been running for two months. It might feel good to hole up for a while.

The next morning a thick frost covered the window. Eva hurried downstairs, following an intoxicating scent of frying potatoes. In the kitchen the woman was at the sink, washing up a few dishes. "Eat if you're hungry," she said. "Ain't no coffee, but there's eggs if you want. Can you cook 'em yourself?"

"Sure. I'd be glad to. Thank you."

She fixed her breakfast while the woman watched. Eva had the feeling she was taking some kind of test.

When she finished eating she took her dishes to the sink and washed them. Then she turned to the woman with an expectant look on her face.

"Can you take care of chickens?" the woman asked.

"Sure. We had them... when my mom was alive." She looked down at the floor as if overcome by her emotions, which in a way she was, but mostly she just hoped she was convincing enough. When she risked a look at the woman she found herself in a staring contest. The old woman finally shook her head and Eva's heart started to sink.

"Well, I can't tell if you're a really good liar or a really bad one, but you don't stink and that's a good sign. Shows you got some self-respect. We don't expect much, Walter and me. We're just trying to get along. You behave yourself, you can stay till spring, if that's what you want to do. You'll take care of the chickens, run errands, feed the pig, clean some. We'll feed you. That's the deal."

Eva grinned. "Thank you! You won't be sorry."

"We'll see."

***

Walter and Madeline Prescott had come to Missouri in the early part of the century, when the internet boom was lifting many boats. Walter was an engineer, skilled at designing useful things. He never quite adapted to the playful side of the web, however, and as the years went by he found himself being passed over while cagier, computer-savvy types proceeded to construct a universe of virtual playgrounds for a population that, for the most part, didn't have to worry about where its next Happy Meal was coming from. But when the Greening pulled the plug and the rug out from under millions of complacent citizens, suddenly Walter found his practical know-how in demand again.

Unfortunately, in the new society widespread lawlessness undermined all efforts to achieve stability, much less progress. Walter and those like him were forced to fashion lives on the border between the used-to-haves and the never-hads. In the last five years Walter had managed to eke out a subsistence, but he had no illusions about a return to what had once passed for normal. The Greening had triggered a disturbing shift in the fundamental chemistry and physics that had once made such beautiful sense of the world to Walter. Now, strange things were happening. Impossible things. Walter knew they should be impossible because he had a degree in the possible.

He looked up from his workbench and watched the new girl poking around the chicken yard. She was quiet, at least. Not like some of the others. There wasn't much to steal anyway. He sighed and glanced out at a shelf of low-hanging purple clouds. In ordinary times they might have signaled more November rain. Now it was hard to say what those clouds carried.

He looked back out the window and went still. The boy had come up out of nowhere and was hanging onto the fence, his grubby fingers poking through the wire, his eyes on the girl.

She had her hands on her hips, no-nonsense style. Looked like she was telling him to get lost, but Walter couldn't be sure. The boy was smiling like a poker player with a bad hand. Walter considered going out to run the boy off, but decided against it. The girl had to learn.

***

Eva frowned at the six brown eggs in her basket. The urge to throw one at that grinning face was strong, but she fought it down. The Prescotts counted on every single egg.

"Where you from?" the boy asked. His voice wasn't a boy's voice.

"None of your business. You better just keep going."

"I'm not in a hurry."

Eva turned her back on him and pretended to be looking for more eggs, even though she knew there couldn't be any more outside the coop.

"You're new here." It wasn't a question.

She turned to face him and said, "So?"

"So why are you here? Are you kin to the Prescotts?"

Eva glared at him. "What makes you so nosy?"

The boy shrugged. "I have an inquiring mind."

Eva pursed her lips. She went to the gate and stepped out, latching it behind her. She started walking to the back door of the house.

"Hey. What's your name?"

"You don't need to know," she called back over her shoulder.

"I'm Clayton. You'll see me again."

Eva shook her head and went into the house.

"Who were you talking to?" Maddy asked.

"Some boy."

Maddy went to the window and stared out for a moment. "Oh," she said, and turned away with a slight frown.

"You know him?" Eva asked.

"Everybody knows him."

"Why?"

Maddy sighed and looked back out the window. "He's an orphan. Looters killed his mama and his daddy. Clayton found the bodies when he came home from school. That was four years ago. He ain't been back to school since."

"What does he do?"

"Hangs around. Asks too many questions."

Eva thought about the bright look in his eyes. "Where does he live?"

"He lives alone in the house where his parents died. They're buried in the backyard."

"How does he get by?"

"He's got a bow. He hunts. He's got a little garden. Grows potatoes like the rest of us."

Eva sat down at the kitchen table. After a few minutes she asked, "How old is he?"

"I reckon he's fourteen now. He had to grow up fast."

Eva considered this as she helped Maddy around the house. She hadn't given much thought to school since she left D.C., but the mention of it made her wonder if she would ever go back to school herself. She felt a pang of wistfulness for that lost age of innocence, when boys mattered, clothes mattered. She wondered if anything would ever be the same.

Sometimes when she lay awake in the night, she reflected on the mystery of her mother's life. Up until she'd found that letter, she'd assumed her mother was just as boring as all the other adults she encountered in her daily life. She had tried to come up with a plausible—forgivable—reason for why her mother had lied about her father. Maybe he was a criminal. Maybe he was a married man whose wife didn't know about Shiloh. Maybe he was a one-night stand, and her mother was ashamed and embarrassed by her misstep. Even if any of these theories were true, none of them was good enough to excuse her mother for lying to her. Yet Eva missed her mother. There was a part of her that wished her mother had a good excuse. Some really good reason why she couldn't tell Eva. Then Eva could forgive her and...

At that point in the monologue Eva hit the wall. She didn't know what she wanted from her mother anymore. And she wasn't ready to forgive and forget.

On the night after her encounter with Clayton, Eva couldn't help comparing her own relatively civilized experience with the brutal tragedy the boy had to overcome. As she recalled the way his eyes sparkled with amusement while he peppered her with questions, she couldn't help feeling impressed by his resilience, and a little ashamed of her unwillingness to be friendly.

The trouble was, since The Greening, being friendly had become a fast route to being dead. Many robbers, looters and rapists were known to employ charming smiles to mask their vile intentions. Young as she was, Eva had already witnessed enough to make her suspicious of anyone who appeared too friendly.

CHAPTER 3

Clayton walked home the long way, on the path that ran beside the river where his mother used to take him when he was a little boy. Not many people used the isolated path anymore. It was too dangerous. Clayton had been mugged on it a few times when he was younger. A young boy living alone appeared an easy target. By the time he turned fourteen he had grown six inches and started carrying a dagger. Not many people bothered him anymore. After an initial outpouring of sympathy when his parents were killed, the locals had given up trying to help him. Strangers were wary of the angular boy who seldom smiled and rarely spoke.

He unlatched the gate and let himself into the small house. He lit a candle and fed some twigs to the ashy embers in the wood stove, coaxing the fire to hiss and snap. Out the window that faced the small backyard he could just make out the two small gravestones, bone white in the starless night. He stared at them while shadows flickered in the quiet gloom.

An owl hooted close by. Clayton looked up at the sound and blinked as if just awakened, caught off-guard like a man in a dream finding himself in the wrong house by the recollection of that girl at the Prescotts. Her gray-green eyes had looked right into him with neither pity nor curiosity. But she had *seen* him. And Clayton realized with a sensation new to him that he wished he could get a better look at her.

He wasn't sure why, exactly. But something told him that girl was worth another glance.

***

The nights were getting longer. The first snows had fallen. Ice glazed the river banks; all the horses wore blankets.

Eva trudged to the market to trade some eggs for flour, wishing, not for the first time, that she had been more careful about where she tied up her horse. Since it had disappeared she had been forced to adjust to getting places on foot.

Her hands were warm in the wool socks Maddy had given her in place of gloves. Eva hadn't packed with foresight when she ran from D.C. She was stamping her feet and shivering when she noticed the flyers tacked up on the plywood side of the miller's booth. Faces stared back at her—young mostly, some older women, a few men. Scrawled on a banner above the flyers was the familiar phrase: "Have you seen me?"

Eva stared at the photos, her stomach clenched, her heart beating unsteadily. No one would recognize her, she told herself. The photo showed a happy face framed by long dark hair, a carefree girl with hopeful light in her eyes.

"Think they'll catch on?"

She whipped around. Clayton stood behind her, a smug look on his face, his red hair poking out from a wool cap.

"I don't know what you're talking about," she snapped.

He snorted. "Yeah. Right. And you're a natural blonde."

"So I dye my hair. So what?"

"So why'd you run? Them posters mean someone wants to find you. How come you don't want to be found?"

"Shhhh." Eva glared at him and took a quick look around. No one was paying any attention to them. "Why do you care? Haven't you got things to do?"

"Nope. I got nothin'. No family, no job, no worries." He stared at her without smiling for a moment. "If I did have a family, I'd want to be with them."

Eva pressed her lips together, clutched her sack of flour and started walking away. Clayton fell into step beside her. He didn't say anything more, just matched his stride to hers.

After a few minutes she stopped abruptly and wheeled to face him. "Listen, you don't know me and you never will. I have reasons for why I left, but they're my business, not yours. Why do you stay here? You don't have family here. You could go someplace better."

Clayton's eyes grew dark, and Eva felt a sudden chill. "All my family's here. There's no place else for me to go."

Eva lost the fire of indignation at that. She took a breath and looked across the empty street. "I ran away because I found out that my mother lied to me about my father. She told me—all my life she told me—that he was dead—that he died before I was born. Then I found out he's been alive all this time."

"Maybe she had a reason. Did you ask her?"

"Why would I do that? She lied to me for twelve years. How can I believe anything she says now?"

Clayton shrugged. "So you didn't."

"I didn't give her the chance to tell me any more lies. I'm gonna find him. Maybe he'll tell me the truth."

"Do you know where he is?"

Eva's shoulders sagged. She kicked at a pile of snow beside the road. "I don't even know his whole name."

Clayton shook his head. "You got half a name?" An amused light flickered in his face, and Eva bit her lip but couldn't prevent a small smile from peeking out.

"Yeah. Half a name's better than nothing, I guess."

Clayton's smile broadened. "Which half is it? The front or the back?"

Eva rolled her eyes. "The front. I guess."

"So what is it?"

"What is what?"

"Your dad's name."

"Forest."

Clayton's face took on a puzzled aspect. "That's better than John or Joe. Not so many Forests out there, I bet."

"I guess."

"How've you been searching? You got a picture of him?"

"No." Eva felt a resurgence of irritation as the boy poked holes in her none-too-carefully-thought-out plan. She started walking again. He kept up.

After another minute she said, "Listen, I know it's crazy to think I'll be able to find him. I mean, he could be dead now for all I know. But... I just had to get away from my mom. I've got to figure this out on my own."

Clayton nodded. "Yeah. I can see that." He stopped walking and watched her take a few steps before she noticed. When she paused and turned to look at him he said, "I get it. You've got to do this by yourself. If you change your mind... if you just want to talk. I'm not going anywhere."

Eva nodded. "Thanks." She left him standing in the road. She didn't look back. He watched her until she was out of sight.

***

On Christmas night Maddy roasted a chicken and opened a can of peaches. She gave Eva a pair of red wool gloves. Walter gave her a heavy Maglite. When she raised her eyebrows at the unexpected gift, he said, "Every girl should carry one of those. Keep it handy."

Eva felt flustered because she hadn't thought to get any gifts for them. She had tried to put Christmas out of her mind, scowling at a group of carolers laughing in the street, singing songs of joy and peace. Yet after she went to bed that night she was overcome with homesickness, thinking of her mother and Josh, the candles and the scent of cookies that would fill the house. She wondered if her mother was thinking of her. Tears sprang to her eyes but she wiped them away furiously and clenched her fists, holding tight to the anger lodged in her gut like shrapnel.

She was lonely. In a few days she would be thirteen. She wished she could talk to someone about the changes happening in her body. But she was too proud and too far down this path to go back now.

She thought of Clayton and wondered how he spent Christmas. Lighting candles at his parents' graves? She had seen him several times since they last spoke, but she tried to avoid him. She felt his eyes following her when she went in town. She even admitted to herself that he was cute. There was no point in pretending otherwise. His air of sadness touched her more than she cared to admit. But she gritted her teeth and hardened her heart.

Late one afternoon on a freezing January day Eva was returning from the barter hall, distracted by the awareness that it was her birthday. She hadn't planned to mention the fact to anyone, but that morning as she passed the calendar tacked on the kitchen wall she had mused aloud, "It's my birthday," unaware that she was in range of Maddy's sharp hearing.

The older woman immediately announced that they would celebrate with a special dinner that night. Eva had tried to discourage this, but she relented when Maddy added that Walter enjoyed cake and they never had it as a rule.

Eva was thinking about how the Prescotts were starting to treat her as if they were her parents when she noticed Clayton standing near the one-room schoolhouse. On impulse she approached him and asked, "School let out early today?"

He looked at her evenly. "I don't go to school."

"Why not? You know everything?"

"I know enough."

"Enough for what? To spend the rest of your life here doing nothing?"

He took a step back and shook his head. "What's it to you?"

"Forget it. None of my business." She started walking past him.

After a half second delay he caught up with her. "What about you? You're not in school."

"It's different for me. I'm not staying here."

He dug his hands deeper in his pockets. "Why not?"

"You know why. I'm gonna find my dad. As soon as the snows let up I'm leaving."

"Where are you going?"

Eva chewed her lip for a moment before she replied. "I don't know yet."

A light snow began falling as they walked away from the town.

"Where do you live, anyway?" she asked.

He pointed west, to a narrow gravel road. "A mile down that way."

She peered in that direction and saw an empty gray horizon, desolate and cold. A dark stretch of leafless forest crowded both sides of the road.

Eva stopped walking and asked Clayton. "Why do you stay there?"

"My parents are there. I can't leave them alone."

"What do you mean? Do you think that's what they'd want? For you to spend your whole life guarding their bones? Don't you think they'd want you to live your life?"

Clayton's expression darkened. "You don't know anything about me or my family."

"I heard you didn't have a family anymore."

He froze, staring at her. She instantly regretted her words and began to apologize, but she had only gotten as far as the words "I'm sorry" when Clayton was suddenly knocked to the ground by a large boy with a knife who appeared out of nowhere from behind him. Two more boys jumped from the woods at the side of the road. One fell upon Clayton, the other leered at Eva and made a grab for her.

She leapt away from him, dropped her bag of supplies, and closed her fist around the Maglite in her pocket.

"Ooh, you want to play, girlie?" the boy sneered, lunging for her.

She brought the Maglite out and smashed it into his face with all her strength. She felt his nose crack on impact and saw blood pour over his face. He roared in pain and dove for her, but she side-stepped him and brought the Maglite down again on the back of his head as he went by. He fell to the ground and stayed there.

She turned to the two boys battering Clayton, who was trying to fight back. Eva swung the Maglite around and slammed it into the head of one of the boys. He slumped away from Clayton, who rolled away from the last boy and gained the upper hand, landing a few blows before the boy noticed his friends out cold in the snow. He shot a furtive glance at Eva, who snarled at him, "That's right. Come on, you little creep."

The boy scrabbled to his feet and ran out of sight.

Eva turned to Clayton and said, "Are you okay?"

He was standing unsteadily, his face bloody and already swelling. She rushed to his side and grabbed him before he could fall. Then she noticed his hand clutching his side and a thin stream of dark blood oozing from his jacket.

"Come on," she said, pulling his arm over her shoulder to take his weight. "We've got to get you to a hospital."

"There's no hospital," he whispered. His face was ashen.

"Okay. New plan. Let's get you home."

She shouldered his weight as best she could and trudged toward the gravel road.

It took much longer than she would have liked. Clayton didn't speak the whole time, though she could hear him sucking in air as if each breath hurt. She peeked inside his jacket at one point to make sure the wound wasn't gushing. Once she was assured that he wouldn't bleed to death before they got him out of the cold, she did her best to keep up a slow, steady march. She was grateful the snow wasn't any deeper.

She tried not to think about the three thugs behind them, hoping that if they planned to renew their attack they would wait a while. She considered asking Clayton if he had a rifle at the house, but she had to focus on putting one foot in front of the other and not letting him fall.

The sun was sinking below the frozen horizon when they reached the small house. The door was locked. "Key in pocket," he mumbled.

She shifted her weight, regained her balance and reached inside his pants pocket to find the key. She unlocked the door and they staggered inside.

She lowered him onto the couch in the living room and lit a candle. Then she turned on the Maglite and shone it on Clayton while she opened his coat and examined the wound. It wasn't as deep as she'd feared, but the gash was wide and ragged. Blood was oozing steadily from it. She looked around the room.

"Do you have any antiseptic? Any clean cloth?" she asked. "It ought to be stitched. I can't do that. But it's got to be cleaned."

She found what she needed in the bathroom and set to work. After she had done what she could, she opened the woodstove and stoked the fire. When she turned back to him his eyes were closed. Her heart skipped a beat.

"Clayton?" she said softly, moving closer.

"I'm alive," he whispered, without opening his eyes.

"Well, stay that way," she said.

He opened one eye and looked at her. "I'll try."

"There is no try," she said.

"What does that mean?" he asked.

She shrugged. "It's just something Josh used to say when I was a kid."

"Who's Josh?"

Eva let out a breath. "My mom's friend." She glanced out the dark window and suddenly remembered Maddy and Walter and the plan for her birthday.

"What?" he asked.

She shook her head. "It's nothing. I just remembered that the Prescotts were expecting me for dinner."

"You should go."

"I can't go. You're hurt. You need someone here."

"I'll be okay."

She felt his forehead. "If that gets infected..."

"I'll be fine."

"I suppose you don't have a phone?"

"No phone. No electricity."

"Great." She frowned and bit her lip. "Okay, here's what's going to happen. I'm going to run home... I mean, to the Prescotts and tell them what happened. I can probably get some better first aid stuff from them. Then I'll come back and stay here tonight."

"Too dangerous. Those guys could still be out there."

"That's all the more reason I have to stay here. Walter can come with me if he thinks I won't be safe. But I will be. If those guys come anywhere near me or you I'll kick their asses. Again."

Clayton attempted a grin.

"I'm going now. I'll be back as fast as I can. I'll lock the door, okay?"

When she moved to stand up he reached for her hand. "Be careful," he said.

She let herself out and locked the door behind her. A sliver of moon was tipping above the treeline as she started jogging down the road.

She came to the turning point in the road after only a short time, and felt a shiver of relief, guessing she was almost halfway. She didn't see the boys until they jumped out of the darkness right in front of her. She tightened her grip on the Maglite, but there were three of them, and faint moonlight glinted on the knife one of the boys brandished at her.

"Where do you think you're going?" he jeered.

Time slowed down inside her head. She knew in some part of her brain that she should be terrified, but she felt calm and cold and clear-eyed. A tide of rage roiled in her chest, but she wasn't in a hurry to take them apart. She felt as if she could see inside their tiny brains, and having sized them up, she knew exactly how to destroy them.

She stood still and watched them the way a cat watches a mouse that has come in clawing range. The boys exchanged looks, as if they hadn't planned the next step in their attack. Eva fixed her eyes on the boy whose nose was clearly broken and waited for him to make the first move. She knew he would.

When he lunged for her with an angry grunt, she kicked him in the crotch and he crumpled to the ground with a surprised scream. The other two boys tried to grab her at the same time. Eva ducked and slipped between them, swiping one of them on the side of the head with the Maglite. He howled in pain and tried to grab her wrist while the other boy turned and punched her face.

The impact of his knuckles on her cheek made Eva bite her tongue, but it didn't hurt as much as she'd expected, a surprise which she might have examined if she hadn't been simultaneously surprised by the bloodcurdling shriek the boy let out at the instant of contact. He hopped away from her, holding his hand and howling as if he'd been burned.

The boy glared at her and whined, "What did you do to me? You got a taser?"

Eva gazed coolly at the three boys, who were gaping at her uncertainly. Then she said, "If you try to touch me again I'll kill you. Understand?"

"What are you? Some kind of witch?" the boy on the ground asked.

"What I am is none of your business. All you need to know is you don't bother me or my friend ever again. Or it will be the last time you bother anyone. Got it?"

The boys mumbled agreement and scuttled back into the darkness.

Eva resumed jogging to the Prescotts. The thought occurred to her that the boys might try again. She considered the fact that she had never killed anyone. *There's a first time for everything*, she mused.

The Prescotts were alarmed when they saw her face. Eva had forgotten the punch already, but she touched her cheekbone and felt the swelling. She explained that she and Clayton had been mugged and that they had fought off their attackers. She didn't mention the second attack.

The Prescotts agreed with her plan to return to Clayton's to keep an eye on him until he was able to manage for himself. They ate the birthday dinner quickly. Afterward Maddy wrapped some food for Eva to take with her, including a large slice of cake. Walter put some first aid supplies in a bag. As he was handing them to her he reached for his coat and said, "I'll come with you."

She put a hand on his arm. "No. That's okay. You don't have to. I'll be fine. Really. I'll come by tomorrow and take care of the chickens."

"Don't worry about them. I can manage for a few days. Take care of the boy," Maddy said. Then she startled Eva by stepping close and giving her a quick hug.

"You be careful," Maddy said.

"I will," Eva said, stepping back into the night.

She started out jogging but slowed down after a few minutes as she reflected that she could hear better if she walked. In the darkness she kept her eyes wide open. The moonlight was thin but the snow intensified it. Eva felt as if she could see for miles.

She arrived at Clayton's house without incident and let herself in. He was lying on the couch in almost the same position he'd been in when she left. She tiptoed close and listened to his breathing. He appeared to be asleep, but when she turned away he whispered, "You came back."

"Did you think I wouldn't?"

"Wouldn't blame you."

She scoonched next to him on edge of the couch, and reached out to feel his forehead. It was dry and cool.

"I'm taking care of you. Get used to it," she said. "Want some of my birthday cake?"

He smiled. "You brought me cake?"

"It's pretty good cake."

He groaned softly, closed his eyes and shifted his body. "Maybe later. Kinda sick to my stomach."

She stared at his face in the candlelight. Without thinking she reached for his hand and held it. He squeezed hers gently, but his eyes stayed closed. After a while his grip relaxed and she sensed that he'd fallen asleep. She stared at him for a long time before she let go of his hand.

***

The next morning she cleaned his wound and tried to get him to eat.

"You don't have to stay here," he said. "I'll be okay."

She shook her head. "What if those guys come back when I'm not around?"

"I'll manage."

She pursed her lips. "Yeah. I've seen how you manage. Not impressed."

"Yeah, well. I was distracted."

"By what?"

He gave her a look. She rolled her eyes and said, "You don't give up, do you?"

He just smiled.

"You're an idiot. You know that?" she said.

His smile changed to something else while he stared at her silently. She held his gaze as long as she could. When she finally turned away she still felt his eyes upon her.

***

By the end of the week Clayton was healed enough that Eva began to feel tense every time he looked at her. Finally she packed the few things she'd brought and told him she was leaving.

He was quiet for a moment. Then he said, "You could stay here."

She shook her head. "No. I really can't."

"Yes, you can. Why don't you?"

"You know why. I'm going to find my dad. Winter will be over soon. I've wasted enough time here." She knew he wouldn't like hearing that, but she had to say it.

His brow furrowed. She could see he was struggling not to say anything. But he did. "You're not gonna find your dad. You know that. He could be anywhere. He could be dead."

A spark of anger lit her eyes for a moment. "Maybe you're right. But maybe you're not. Anyway, it's not your problem. I'm not gonna stay here and play house with you."

Clayton lowered his chin and gazed into her eyes. "It might be fun."

She snorted softly. "Yeah. Well. I'm sure there are lots of girls around here who would be glad to... play with you. You'll be fine."

He straightened up and shrugged his shoulders.

As she opened the door she turned and said, "Take care of yourself."

"Why should I?" he shot back.

She focused on him then and took a long breath before she said, "For me. Do it for me."

He smiled slightly. "Okay. I'll do it for you."

She smiled then and said in a lighter tone, "Thanks. Who knows? I might need you one day."

Then she leaned closer to him and kissed him quickly on the cheek before she disappeared out the door.

***

Clayton went over to the couch and sank onto it, numb. After a while he looked around the room. It was still exactly the same as it had been ever since his parents died. But now the small cozy room seemed emptier than ever before. The clock ticked on the mantel beside the fading photo of his parents from their wedding day. He stared at it and felt his chest contract in pain.

Everywhere he looked he saw Eva, though she had left no trace behind. He should have asked her for something to remember her by. He hung his head and laughed at himself.

Yeah, like you're going to forget her.

CHAPTER 4

For the next few weeks as the snows continued and the dark nights left her far too much time to think, Eva tried to figure out a way to speed up her search. *At this rate I'll be grown up before I find him*, she thought.

She took to hanging around the stables where the mail coaches stopped to rest and take care of their horses. She asked the same question of every stranger passing through. "Do you know a man named Forest?"

The ones who bothered to answer usually said no. Of the few who said yes she asked more questions, only to learn that the Forests they knew were old men, or too young to be her father. She began to wish she'd stayed in D.C. long enough to learn more about her father, so that she'd have more to go on. But she couldn't go back now. Her mother would probably put her under lock and key.

One balmy day in late February, Eva wandered down by the river. The ice was starting to crack and thin. A wash of milky sunlight filtered through the hazy sky. She felt a rush of eagerness to get going again. But where? She reached down to the pebbly shore and picked up a flat oval stone. Absently she threw it toward a stretch of muddy open water. But when the stone touched the surface, instead of skipping a few times it transformed into a small silvery fish that leapt briefly in the air and then vanished under the water.

Eva stared at the spot. After a half minute she bent down and selected another stone. She held it in the palm of her hand for a moment, staring at it as if to confirm that it was an ordinary stone. Then she tossed it as she'd tossed the other. Again, the stone skipped once along the water and rose with scales, gills and fins flashing in the pearly reflected light before it dived under the surface.

Eva frowned and glanced behind her. If some jackass was messing with her she was going to be pissed. But there was no one around. The wooded path that led to this stretch of the bank was empty.

Eva shook herself and reached for another, larger, stone. "Okay," she muttered. "Third time's a charm." She aimed for the deeper part of the river. The stone sailed like a bird until it touched the water, then it wriggled and spun its fishy form in the air for a dripping instant before diving out of sight.

"Shit," Eva whispered.

"You need a net."

She turned her head slowly and saw a woman standing at the edge of the woods watching her.

Eva hesitated for a second, but the woman didn't look armed or crazy, so she said, "I don't know what just happened."

"You made a fish. If you had a net you could make dinner."

"It was a fish?"

"What'd you think it was?"

"I... I wasn't sure. That never happened before."

The woman stared at Eva as if she were a live bomb to be defused. The woman looked to be in her thirties, but the squint in her eyes made her appear older. She wore faded blue jeans, a dark blue puffy nylon jacket and hiking boots. Wavy reddish brown hair spilled out from her black knit cap.

"You're not from around here, are you?" she asked.

Eva pursed her lips. She'd heard this question, or similar versions of it, everywhere she went. "I'm here now. Just like you," she said, staring back at the woman.

The woman nodded and straightened up, seeming to have arrived at some decision. "You know, not everybody can do that kind of thing."

"What? Make fish out of stones?"

Something altered in the woman's expression. "Yeah." She looked behind her and then back at Eva. "How old are you?"

"How old are you?" Eva shot back.

"If I had to guess I'd say you were thirteen. Maybe fourteen, but you're kinda small."

Eva grimaced. The last year had brought a lot of unwelcome changes in her body. Unlike most of her former girlfriends, she hadn't been looking forward to getting breasts and all that went with them. Boys were annoying enough already. But there was no hiding the fact that she was growing, and not all of it was up.

She sighed. "I turned thirteen last month," she said.

The woman nodded. "I thought so. That would explain the fish."

"How?" Eva demanded.

"Come on," the woman said. "There's someone you ought to meet."

Eva reached for another rock—a bigger one, and hefted it in her hand while she said, "I'm not following you anywhere unless you tell me who you are and what you want with me. I'm not stupid."

"I can see that," said the woman. "My name is Elvira. My husband and I got a commune nearby. We raise goats, pigs, a few horses. We take in people who need a place to stay, let 'em work for their keep. We're good people. Not slave traders."

"Maybe you can help me. I'm looking for my father. His name is Forest. You seen anybody with that name?"

The woman shrugged. "Might have. We see a lot of folks passing through."

Eva tossed the rock back and forth between her hands, sensing something off in the woman's tone of voice. She was pretty sure the woman wasn't telling her the whole truth, but on the other hand, she hadn't seemed a bit surprised by the fish. If Eva'd had a coin she might have tossed it, but as it was she muttered, "What the hell," and dropped the rock on the muddy bank, where it sprouted legs and a tail and scurried into the brush.

Eva looked up at the woman, who grinned and said, "Tails it is."

Eva gaped at her.

"Come on. This way." Elvira marched back into the woods. Eva hesitated only a heartbeat before following.

***

After a half-hour drive over a dry dirt road Elvira pulled the horse to a stop in front of a rundown white farmhouse. She hadn't spoken since they set out, and Eva had resisted the temptation to ask questions, although she wondered what the woman had been doing by the river. The wagon was loaded with hay bales.

Elvira hopped down and looked up at Eva. "Don't get any ideas about driving off," she said.

"Where would I go?"

"How do I know? You're the one looking for somebody."

Eva climbed down and peered at the bare fields stretching beside the house. "What do you grow here?" she asked.

"Used to be corn. Soybeans. Some potatoes. Now..." the woman shrugged. "We're trying to keep a few goats. We'll see how it goes." She tilted her head toward the house. "Come on."

It wasn't much warmer inside, but the woman led Eva through the dark and chilly living room to a smaller room at the back of house where the murmur of voices came from behind a closed door. Elvira knocked on it.

"Yeah?" said a man's voice.

She opened the door and stepped in. Eva stopped in the doorway. There were two men and one woman in the room. The older of the men stared at her before turning his gaze to Elvira.

"I found this girl at the river," she said. "This is Daniel. That's Carl, that's Missy."

Eva kept her eyes on Daniel, whose stare was creeping her out.

"And what do they call you?" he said. There was an edge to his voice that gave Eva the feeling he didn't expect her to give him her real name, nor did he care.

"They call me Angela."

He nodded. "What brings you here?"

"She's looking for her daddy."

"What's he look like?" Daniel asked.

Eva let out a long breath and glanced up at the ceiling before she replied. "I don't know."

Carl snorted. Daniel held up a hand to silence him. "When was the last time you saw him?" he asked.

"I've never seen him, okay? I didn't know he existed until a few months ago. Now I'm trying to find him."

Daniel nodded. "What do you know about him?"

"I know his name is Forest. His first name."

"That's it?" Missy asked.

Eva glowered at them all. "Listen. She told me you might be able to help. If you can't, I'll be on my way."

Daniel looked at Elvira then, and Eva saw something register between them. Elvira told Missy and Carl to come into the kitchen with her.

After they'd left Daniel said, "You want to sit down?"

"No thanks. Don't think I'm staying."

"Listen. I'm sorry if Elvira got your hopes up. A lot of people come through here looking for one thing or another. Sometimes we can help. Sometimes we can't. Maybe if you tell us a little more about your father..."

"I don't know anything more," she snapped. "If I did, I wouldn't be here."

Daniel turned his stare out the window with a slight frown. "If you don't want our help you're free to go."

Eva scowled. "It's a long walk back to town."

"I'm sorry. I can't send the wagon back until we have another load to trade."

"When will that be?"

"The day after tomorrow if we're lucky."

Eva dropped into one of the empty chairs. "Fine," she muttered. She could feel Daniel's eyes on her again. She met his gaze and said, "Would you stop doing that?"

He stared a moment longer, then turned away and said, "You remind me of someone." He shook his head as if to clear it. "A lot of people pass through here on their way west."

Eva leaned back in her chair and glanced around the room. Maps of Montana, North Dakota and Missouri covered most of one wall. Portions of each map were marked in shades of orange, green and purple. She couldn't make sense of it.

"Didn't your mother ever talk about your father?"

"No. She told me he died before I was born."

"But you believe he's alive?"

"I don't know. I only know my mom lied to me. And I'm gonna find out the truth."

His focus grew sharper as he studied her for another moment. "What does your mother do?"

Eva shrugged impatiently. "I don't know. She travels a lot. She's always gone. She never talks about her job." She sighed. "I guess she makes good money. I don't want to talk about her."

"Okay. I just thought maybe... maybe if she did keep the truth from you... maybe she had a good reason. Parents sometimes try too hard to protect their kids."

"Yeah. Maybe. All I know is, I'm not a little kid, and she should have told me about my dad."

He was staring at her again. She shook her head and almost smiled. "Cut it out," she said.

"Oh. Sorry. It's just... I'm trying to think who you remind me of."

"Yeah well, everybody looks like somebody. Whoever it was, I'm not her, okay?"

"Right. It's just... your voice, too." He frowned and a clouded look came into his eyes. Then he sat up straighter and said, "Listen, why don't you go on in the kitchen and find something to eat. You can sleep in the girls' room—we've got sort of a dorm situation for kids passing through. If that's okay."

She stood up, relieved to be dismissed. "Sure. That's fine."

"And we'll send you back to town as soon as we can."

She shrugged. "Okay. No worries."

After she left the room, Daniel stared into space trying to chase down a memory stirring in the depths of his mind. He couldn't have seen her before. She was much too young. But her voice, the shape of her face, the quickness in her eyes echoed someone he'd met... but whenever he tried to summon that face the image of Elvira stood in the way, like a blackout curtain over a window. He closed his eyes and leaned his head on his hands.

"You all right?"

He hadn't heard her come in. She had the healer's way of moving soundlessly. It was one of the things that he liked about her, although at this moment he would have preferred to be left alone to find his lost memory. But he looked up and she smiled at him in her easy way, a smile that seemed to suggest everything would be fine. He smiled back.

"Yeah. I'm fine. That girl looks like someone, but I can't think who."

Elvira nodded and said, "Well, we see so many folks, that's only natural." She ran a hand through his hair and sat down beside him. "So what do you think, should we keep her?"

"Oh I don't think we could even if we wanted to." He laughed softly. "She seems pretty determined. Kids that age..." His eyes widened and a light came into his face. "Shiloh. That's who it was. That's who that girl looks like. I mean, the hair's wrong, but the face..." He fell silent, his gaze gone inside.

Elvira stiffened and pulled her hand away, watching him carefully. "Well now, it's probably just your imagination. Everybody wanted to find that girl back in the day. But the government has her now, so we're all safe. You don't have to worry."

"I'm not worried," Daniel insisted. He paused and continued in a more level tone. "It's just, you know? Maybe she had a kid. That girl...she has the same kind of fire inside." He paused again. "I wish I could help her."

Elvira watched him for another minute. Then she reached for the pendant hanging at her neck and said in a soothing tone, "Maybe the best thing we can do is just send her on her way."

Daniel continued speaking as if he hadn't heard her. "Shiloh was on a mission too. She was taking her father back to North Carolina, and she was trying to keep the magic from spreading, just like we are. Only she understood what was going on before anybody else figured it out."

"Huh," sniffed Elvira. "That's because she was mixed up with those terrorists who started it."

"They weren't terrorists. Or at least, she wasn't."

Elvira held her tongue, with some effort. After another moment she said, "Daniel, I don't think we should let this girl stay here. It's too dangerous. If she is who you think she is, trouble's gonna come looking for her. And we got enough of that as it is."

"But if she is Shiloh's child, Shiloh must be looking for her. We should keep her here until Shiloh comes."

Elvira managed a thin smile. She reached out and put her left hand on Daniel's arm while she grasped the pendant in her right. "Dan'l, you know I love you, and I would do anything in my power to help you. But I don't think keeping this little girl here is the right thing for us. We have to think about all the people who are counting on us to guide them through these dangerous times. This girl—she may be who you think she is, or she may be just another runaway breaking some poor mother's heart—whoever she is, we got enough on our plate now. I say we send her on her way, and wish her good luck. That's all we can do. I'm right about this Dan'l. You trust me. I know what's best."

As she stroked her words into his skin Daniel slipped back into himself and grew quiet. When she finished he nodded.

"All right. You know what's best."

She patted his head and left the room. Eva stood waiting at the doorway.

"So you know what's best, huh?"

Elvira glared at her. "I do what's best for me and mine. You're trouble."

"Oh yeah? You're one to talk. Don't worry. I'm leaving. But this isn't over."

Outside the house Eva looked around and saw a horse grazing in a field by the barn. She slipped past the house, climbed on the horse and rode off into the twilight.

***

He never should have let her leave. *As if I could have stopped her*, he thought.

In the long hours between dusk and dawn Clayton's thoughts constantly returned to how it had felt having Eva in the house during that week while he was recovering from the attack. Everything had been different when she was around. The house hadn't seemed so small, or dark, or cold. Since she had gone he had tried to tell himself it never could have worked out. She was just a kid. And so was he.

It didn't matter. He wanted her back.

Yet when he finally worked up the nerve to go to the Prescotts to see if he could persuade her to stay, he learned that she had already left.

"She didn't tell us she was leaving," Mrs. Prescott said, pursing her lips.

"We knew she wasn't going to stay," Mr. Prescott said, coming up beside her.

"That may be, but she could have said goodbye," Mrs. Prescott said with an air of disapproval.

"Maybe she wanted to, but she didn't have a chance," Mr. Prescott suggested.

"Well, we'll never know," said Mrs. Prescott. She looked at Clayton and asked, "Are you all right out there by yourself?"

He nodded. "Yes, ma'am. I'm fine. I just wondered if she was still here. She told me she was leaving soon. Guess she went."

He trudged back to the road and turned toward home, his feet slowing with each step, as he thought about the empty house that awaited him. It hadn't seemed so empty in the four years before he met Eva. Faced with the prospect of going back to the way things had been before then, he found himself thinking of the dark time right after his parents had been murdered. For the first few months he had been unable to allow himself to think about them at all. It was all he could do to stay moving, in the present moment. If he looked back into the chasm of the past he knew he would fall and fall until there would be no way to climb back into his own life. Yet gradually, as days folded into weeks and weeks gathered into months, months piled into years and memories were safely locked behind the bars of time.

This time though it was a different kind of loss, a narrowing of his future, a closing in of the possibilities open to a young man. At first he wouldn't allow himself to dwell on this feeling, but though he could force his mind not to wander in the daytime, at night his dreams burst all boundaries. In them he lay with Eva, his flesh hot and hungry against hers. The dreams were so vivid he could smell her hair, hear her laugh, taste her lips. He awoke drained and exhausted, gazing around the dark room like a sailor lost at sea.

When he finally gave in to his hope and went to the Prescotts and learned that she had gone he felt as if he'd run into a stone wall. He stumbled home in a daze. He entered his parents' house and looked around, seeing it as she must have seen it. *No wonder she didn't stay.* His glance fell as usual upon the photo on the mantel of his parents, a faded color snapshot of them from their wedding. They looked so happy, the way he wanted to think of them always. He turned away from the picture and noticed the guitar case tucked in the shadows of the corner where it had sat untouched since his father's death.

When Clayton was a little boy, maybe eight or nine, his father had tried to teach him to play. The boy's hands had been too small then, and he became discouraged. But as he stared at the case he remembered how his father used to play and sing for his mother. The happiness of that time seemed surreal to Clayton now.

Without thinking Clayton grabbed the case and moved to the couch. He pulled out the guitar and tried a chord. It was out of tune and the strings were rusty, but just putting his arms around the guitar gave Clayton an unexpected sense of comfort. He leaned into it, tuned the strings, and tried again. The sound was raw and rough, yet something inside the boy resonated with the guitar's voice and rose to meet it like a new sun lifting in an empty sky.

He leaned back and tried to remember everything his father ever showed him.

And when he'd done that, he rummaged around and found a set of new strings and few music books. When night fell, he lit a candle and continued picking out melodies, until the empty house began to fill with a new warmth, and a new light burned in Clayton's eyes.

Chapter 5

Shiloh trudged past the BMW planter on the corner of 28th and Q Street.

Daffodils were already blooming where the engine used to be. Spring seemed to come earlier and earlier. Whether because of global warming or the planet's own timetable for seasons, Shiloh neither knew nor cared.

The car planter was one of the few remaining relics of the gas-fueled auto age in the city. Nearly all the ruined cars had been stripped and carried off by gangs of metalheads who traded the scraps for more useful commodities such as food or weapons or drugs. The fact that the BMW's owner had made her car into an ad hoc garden site struck Shiloh as ironic, considering that the entire city was now overrun with weeds and vines. But she had to admit the flowers blooming in the open trunk were a welcome sight after a week spent tracking a self-styled wizard through the snows of Alberta.

On the brick walk to the townhouse she noticed the light in the window. She forced down the knee-jerk reflex of hope that assailed her every time she came home. Eva would not be there. If she were, Josh would have sent her a message. She went in and dropped her bags. The scent of roasted chicken with a touch of tarragon woke her stomach from its sullen stillness.

Josh came out from the kitchen, took a look at her, and stepped closer for a hug. She turned away and side-stepped him.

"Sorry," she muttered. "I just... I'm worn out."

He stopped smiling. "Of course you are. Are you hungry? I've got dinner ready."

She attempted a smile. "Yeah. That'd be good." She followed him back to the kitchen. The table was set, candles lit, salad ready. The room had a warm, cozy glow. Gazing around as the light faded from the sky outside Shiloh was struck by how this place had come to feel like home, even though it had never been something she chose. One thing had just led to another. Josh was alone when she met him the second time, and he had been so helpful and generous. She watched him filling a plate for her and felt the usual stab of guilt. What had he given up to be a part of her life? If she hadn't moved in, maybe he would have found someone to cook for him. And more.

He deserved more, she knew, but she'd never asked him to give up anything for her. If he'd brought home a woman and told Shiloh to move out, she would have. But he wasn't looking for anyone else. And she resented how guilty that made her feel.

"You know you didn't have to do this, right? I can take care of myself."

"I know. I like to cook for you." He poured them each a glass of wine, a rare and precious commodity since trade and transportation had become so difficult.

"Are we celebrating something?" she asked.

He shrugged. "I'm just glad you're back." He looked into her eyes and she shrank away from the naked desire in his gaze.

As if he sensed her reluctance, he sat back and said in a heartier tone, "Well, how'd it go? Where were you?"

She gulped some wine and let out a long breath. "Oh, you know. The usual. Crazy kids hopped up on magic trying to rule their little worlds. Same old, same old."

Josh nodded, but the light in his eyes glinted with something else. She leaned toward him. "What?" she asked. "Did you find something?"

He tilted his head. "Maybe. It might be nothing. But you know we haven't had any leads for months and—"

"What?"

"I got an email response from one of the flyers. Some guy in Missouri says he met a girl who might have been Eva. But she ran away from there. Took one of his horses, he says."

"Show me the email."

"Don't you want to eat first?"

"What do you think?"

He went for his laptop. He handed it to her and watched as she read the message.

"His name is Daniel," she said.

"Does that mean something to you?"

"Maybe. I met a guy... before she was born. He was in North Dakota or something. Sort of a leader, seemed like a good guy."

"And you think this might be him?"

"I don't know." She sighed heavily. "It's been almost five months. I don't know what else to do. I was thinking of going to Magda and asking her to try the vision cauldron, but I don't know if that would work, and I really don't want to go back there."

"Why not? If she's got some magic way of finding people, that makes a lot of sense to me. I don't understand why you didn't go to her in the first place."

"You don't know her. I don't want her having anything to do with Eva."

Josh shook his head. "Well, maybe I'm crazy, but that just seems stupid to me. If you really want to find her and you know someone who has a tool that could help, why wouldn't you use it?"

Shiloh glared at him. "You know nothing about this. Magda is a powerful ruler who's used to getting what she wants. She wanted me. I only got away because of the mess Jack made here. Eva is young and beautiful and innocent. She'd be no match for Magda. There's no way in hell I'm letting Magda go after my child."

"Hey! Don't get mad at me. I'm on your side."

"Yeah, well, fat lot of good that's been."

Josh blanched. He put down his wine glass and said, "What do you mean by that?"

"Oh come on. You know what I mean."

"No. I guess I don't. Why don't you explain it to me?"

Shiloh frowned. "Don't make this about you. You know I'm grateful to you for helping me all these years. But the most important person in my life is Eva. I trusted you to keep her safe. And now she's gone."

In the silence that followed, all the warmth went out of the room. Josh held perfectly still for a moment before he said, "And that's my fault?"

"Well, it's not mine."

"Oh no. Of course not. How could it be your fault? You have more important things to do than be a mother to your own daughter."

The slap of her hand on his face sounded like a gunshot.

He touched his cheek and said quietly, "I'm the one who's been here for Eva, every day when she got up, every day when she went to school, every day when she came home. I'm the one she talked to about her life, about the girls who were mean to her, the boys who were silly around her. Do you even know who Brett Mitchell is?"

"Okay. I get your point. But that doesn't make me a bad parent. I'm just... like lots of working parents. I have to put my job first. That's why I need you."

The light in Josh's eyes turned dark. "Right. Maybe you should find someone else to keep house for you, if you're not satisfied with my work."

He started walking out of the room. "Good luck finding anyone. And that includes Eva. You wouldn't know her if you found her."

"How can you say that?"

He turned at the door and looked at her for a moment. "You know," he said in a quiet tone, "I used to hope that one day you'd... yeah. Guess that just shows how stupid a guy can be. Maybe you should find someplace else to live. If Eva shows up here, I'll send her to you. Though I can't promise she'll go to you. I don't think I would, if I were your kid."

Shiloh stared after him, her guts roiling with anger. She picked up the half-full wine glass and threw it aganst the wall.

Josh glanced at the wine running down the drywall. He shook his head and left the room without another word.

Shiloh sank into her chair as she heard Josh's footsteps going upstairs. She looked back at the email on the screen and quickly tapped in a response.

CHAPTER 6

She was wading in shallow tidewater, her pants rolled up, the sun hot on her back, when the crabs started pinching her toes. She kicked to get them off and woke with a start, clutching the branch to which she'd tied herself the night before to keep from falling out of the tree.

Her foot was still asleep, stinging as the blood flowed back into it. Eva shifted carefully and gazed down at the base of the tree. The horse was still there. She took a deeper breath and let it out slowly. The air was cold, but there was a hint of spring, even this close to the mountains. For the past few days she had been able to see them on the horizon.

She edged around the crotch between the branch and trunk, preparing to slither down, when a sudden whooshing sound roared close by. She froze and peered between the branches to the meadow beside the grove. At first she couldn't make out anything, but as she strained to focus on a rustle in the tall meadow grass there was another loud whooshing sound in the air. Eva held her breath and hoped like hell it was a hot air balloon.

No such luck.

The dragon was greenish gold and medium-sized, its wing span maybe thirty feet across. It thumped to the ground and let out a short burst of sulphurous fire, a finishing touch to the flame-broiled deer in the grass. Eva glanced down at the horse, now pawing wildly at the ground and attempting to break free. If the dragon caught wind of the mare...

Eva dropped to the ground, untied the horse, and quickly led her back the way they'd come, deeper into a small stand of woods near the foothills of the Rockies. She prayed they were downwind of the dragon. She was about to get on the horse and attempt to make a run for it, but as they came to the narrow stream they'd crossed the day before, the mare got spooked by something and bolted across the stream and out of sight.

Eva looked back in the direction of the dragon, wondering what she could do to create a diversion if the dragon came after her. She was staring at the edge of the woods when she thought she saw a strange shimmer between the trees. She blinked her eyes a couple of times, staring harder. The thing didn't go away, though it seemed to vanish if she turned her head. She took a few steps closer, keeping her eyes glued to the wavering slice of air between the trees.

When she was so close she could see that the thing didn't appear to be solid, she extended her right arm and tried to touch it. Her hand vanished inside the milky vapor. She gasped and pulled it back out quickly. "What the hell?" she muttered.

She might have tried a few more experiments, perhaps tossing a stone into the vapor, or attempting to plant a foot inside, but at that moment the dragon roared into view above. It hovered over her, so close she was able to look directly into its golden eyes. For an instant she felt something, a spark of recognition that passed so quickly she later thought she'd imagined it. Then the heat of the dragon's breath blew all hesitation from her mind. She leaped into the shimmering vapor.

The world disappeared. She was standing in a cloud of milky fog. She put her hands out like a blind man, but connected with nothing solid. She tried a step. Then another. The warm damp air smelled like the locker room of a public swimming pool. Eva fought a sense of panic. Her throat was tight, sweat running down her neck.

And then she heard footsteps—running footsteps, coming closer. She sprinted away from the sound, breathing hard. Suddenly out of the corner of her eye she saw a sliver of light winking from a slit in the foggy cloud. She hesitated for a second. The footsteps were getting closer, louder.

She took a gulp of air and pushed through the slit in the fog, and stopped short, blinking in blazing sunlight. She was in a baking red desert. She looked behind for the opening through which she'd come, but she couldn't see any sign of it. She waved her hands through the air, feeling for it, before she remembered the footsteps and yanked her hands back to her sides. The landscape looked something like how she imagined Arizona—flat scrubby terrain, boulders, cactus, distant purple mountains, no sign of human habitation, though as she gazed at one of the taller branched cactus she had the oddest feeling that it was staring back. A scruffy tumbleweed rolled by her ankle, although there was no wind. The intense heat felt good to Eva after a cold night spent in a tree. With no idea where she was, she still felt the need to keep moving, so she set out toward the mountains.

She'd been walking for perhaps half an hour when a guttural voice behind her snarled something in a language she didn't understand. She whipped around and saw a man right behind her. He was dressed in classic barbarian style, all muscles with a side of loincloth. A curved knife hung from the leather strapped across his chest. His hair was coiled in a serpents' tangle of reddish braids, his skin the color of pomegranate. She hadn't heard him approach.

"What do you want?" she demanded, trying to sound fierce.

The man grumbled something and took a step closer.

Eva's fear spiked up a notch but she guessed she might have the edge if it came to a foot race. She spun around and launched herself to get a headstart.

The man lurched after her, and she was dismayed to realize he was surprisingly quick. She didn't dare turn her head, but she could hear him breathing and his heavy feet thudding.

Suddenly his brawny arm closed around her neck and lifted her off the ground. Eva rammed an elbow into his gut and started kicking. When she connected with his skin there was a loud sizzle, and the man let go with a grunt. He stepped away and stared at her, squinting as if trying to read something in her face. He seemed to be a man of few words, content to glare at her, as if waiting for her to take the conversational lead. She was about to say something when another similarly clad man appeared from out of nowhere and started talking to the first one. They grunted back and forth, gesturing repeatedly at her, and Eva found her fear transmuting into a mix of amusement and impatience.

After a couple of minutes she cleared her throat and said, "Okay guys, is this a private game or can anyone play?"

At the sound of her voice the men stopped talking, exchanged a quick glance, turned to her and executed slight bows.

Eva raised her eyebrows. "Really?" she said. She tried unsuccessfully to hide a smile. She returned the bow, and said with as straight a face as she could manage, "Take me to your leader."

The men looked at each other, apparently unfamiliar with the protocol. However, after a few more minutes of grunting and gesturing, they conveyed their desire to lead Eva somewhere, and she, having nothing more pressing on her schedule, followed.

Their pace was brisk. Eva was sweating freely by the time they led her beneath a stone arch into a compound surrounded by boulders. In the shade of one of them several men sat on the ground.

One man, striking for his sheer aura of ferocity, rose at their approach and exchanged a few words with her escort. Then he turned his sharp eyes on her. Eva tried to stand taller. She was wondering how she could communicate with him when he spoke in deeply accented English. "Who are you?"

Eva considered the question for a second. "My name is Eva. I'm searching for my father."

"You are not of this country. Why are you here?"

Eva frowned. "Like I said, I'm looking for my father."

The man returned the frown with interest. "Why are you here?" he repeated.

Eva threw up her hands in exasperation. "How many times do I have to say it? I'm looking for my father."

"You are in the wrong place."

"Maybe so. Look, if you won't help me, is there someone else around here who can?"

The man stared at her for a long minute. Then he turned to the men who'd brought her and said something that sounded like a command. One of the men made a grab for Eva's arm, but the instant his hand touched her skin a sizzling sound ripped through the still air. All the men stepped back and looked from her to their leader.

He raised his eyebrows slightly and said, "So. You are a sorceress. Yet you can't find your own father?"

"I'm not a..." Eva hesitated. "I'm just a... junior sorceress. I won't hurt you. Unless I have to."

A spark flashed in the leader's eyes. "So. 'Junior sorceress.' Perhaps Magda will find you amusing."

"Who is Magda?"

"Magda is ruler of the mountains. I am Rufio, ruler of the Red Plains." He gazed at her for another long moment as if she were a small fish caught in his net, too small to eat, but perhaps not completely worthless. Bait is always useful.

Eva remained silent, hoping that the less he knew about her the better her chances of getting to this Magda person, who might be more sympathetic.

"Can you ride?" Rufio asked.

"You mean horses?"

He nodded once.

"Of course," she replied.

Rufio barked another command. Moments later two men appeared on horseback, leading a fine dappled gray mare.

"My men will take you to Magda's land."

She climbed onto the horse and a bud of hope swelled in her chest. It was a beautiful horse, and on its back she felt secure and in control for the first time in weeks. She smiled brightly at Rufio as they started heading toward the mountains. "Aren't you going to wish me luck?" she asked.

"Luck is the hope of fools. If I thought you a fool, you wouldn't be on my horse."

Eva nodded, but kept her mouth shut. No sense spoiling things.

They rode for hours before stopping by a shallow silver stream threading between black rocks. The mountains were closer, but the light was fading from the sky. The men hopped down from their horses and gestured for Eva to do the same.

"I take it we aren't there yet," she said.

They ignored her while they gathered brush and built a fire. As the sun quickly dropped behind the mountains, the air grew sharply colder. Eva moved closer to the fire. One of the men offered her a portion of what appeared to be dried meat. She wrinkled her nose in distaste, but her stomach was knotted with hunger, so she did her best to chew the tough jerky before she swallowed it. When the darkness fell upon them, the men stretched out beside the fire. As Eva shivered in the gathering shadows, she reflected on the realization that she had no idea where she was or where she was going. She stared up at the stars and wondered if they were the same stars that shone back home. But thinking about home only rekindled the anger that kept her going. *I don't need a home. When I find my father I can stay with him.*

At dawn they set off again. They rode for hours, stopping only to feed and water the horses. Eva was so hungry she actually hoped there would be more of that dried meat, but though the men encouraged her to drink from the streams whenever they rested, they didn't offer any more food.

As the day wore on Eva began to wonder if they would be stopping for another night, but when the light began fading from the sky, they passed through a gap in the foothills and a dramatic vista opened up before them. Dark stony mountains rose abruptly from the desert floor. The men slowed their pace as they led the horses toward a break in the scrubby forest that fringed the lower edges of the mountains. There a narrow path wound upward through the trees. They followed it as the darkness deepened. The air rapidly grew colder the higher they climbed. Eva tried to peer into the woods on either side of the trail, but it was too dark to see anything beyond the rider in front of her.

After what seemed like an hour, they emerged into a clearing overlooking a precipice. There were lights twinkling far below, but what riveted Eva's attention was the enormous castle looming straight ahead. They rode to a massive gate, where the men dismounted and waited.

The gate swung open almost immediately. Eva waited for the men to lead the way inside, but they gestured for her to go on alone. When she hesitated, they took the reins of her horse from her and one of the men gave her a shove.

"That's it? You're leaving?" she asked.

They waited impassively.

Eva stood perplexed for a moment, wondering if she was supposed to just walk right in without an invitation. Then the men turned to leave. She shrugged and started in. As she stepped into the courtyard, the only sound was the water splashing in a magnificent stone fountain carved in the image of a dragon.

She was staring up at the light streaming from the balconies that overlooked the courtyard when she heard a woman's voice.

"I've been expecting you," said the woman. She was tall and stunning. Dark sapphires glimmered in her raven hair, and she carried a scepter molded in a dragon design.

"Are you Magda?"

The woman smiled. "And you are Evangeline, the promised child."

Eva stared. "How do you know about me?"

Magda came closer. She put an arm around Eva's shoulder and said, "Oh my dear, I've known about you since before you were born. I've been waiting for you."

Eva shrugged out of Magda's arm and said, "Oh yeah? Well I never heard of you until yesterday, so a little less with the touchy-feely. How do you know about me? Do you know where my father is?"

Magda sighed, took a step back, and looked Eva up and down. "You do look like your mother," she said.

"If you're trying to win me over, talking about my mother isn't gonna do it. I'm looking for my father."

"I know. And you'll find him. But not tonight. Tonight we'll get you fed and settled in. Perhaps you'd like a bath? Tomorrow we'll discuss what you want, and you will have choices to make. You'd be smart to think carefully about what it is you really want, and what you're willing to do to get it."

Two serving women appeared out of the shadows. Magda told them to take Eva to her room and give her whatever she required.

"I'll see you in the morning. Sleep well. We'll have much to discuss on the morrow," said Magda, sweeping out of sight.

Eva stared after her for a few seconds, but the quippy response she might have made was overruled by the growling of her stomach. *Eat first, fight later.*

CHAPTER 7

Shiloh stepped from the vent into a cloud of white blossoms. The trees seemed to stretch as far as she could see. She didn't recognize them, but she figured they had to be natives, not some kind of magically enhanced hybrid. The Hexcaliber was cool as a clam on her skin.

She started making her way westward, hoping to come upon a road or trail that would allow her to get oriented. Daniel's email had named a small town, but the vent system wasn't particularly helpful beyond major cities. She'd tried to get as close as she could.

After an hour of tramping through woodlands and meadows lit with spring wildflowers she came to a weed-covered track that looked as if it had once been a gravel road. She considered trying to call Daniel, but she didn't want to give him too much advance notice. She didn't want to risk spooking Eva if she was still nearby.

When she came to an abandoned gas station, she stepped over the broken glass and twisted car parts strewn near the door and saw an old rack of mildewed maps in the corner. She found one for Hannibal, but it wasn't much help. Daniel had told her the name of the crossroad nearest his farm, but she didn't know what road she was on. She pawed through stuff piled under the counter and found an old bill with the address of the gas station. "Bingo," she muttered softly. Within a few minutes of studying the map she was out on the gravel road, headed back the way she'd come.

It was a balmy evening by the time she stood outside the weathered gate of what she hoped was Daniel's place. The rundown farmhouse looked in need of paint and a new roof, but there were a couple of dogs on the porch, which suggested that they were doing all right. If they could afford to feed dogs, they weren't starving.

She peered up at the windows, wondering if Eva was staring out at her from one of them. Even though Daniel had said she'd moved on, Shiloh couldn't stifle the hope that her daughter was still there.

She walked up to the house and lifted her hand to knock on the screen door. The door behind it opened. A bearded slender man, neither old nor young, stared at her through the screen. Then he said, "Shiloh."

She recognized the voice, its resonant depth summoned a memory of chiseled cheekbones and deep-set eyes from thirteen years before. "Daniel," she said.

"Come in," he said.

She stepped past him and felt a sharp burn from the Hexcaliber resting below her throat. She glanced quickly at him, but his face was unreadable, even this close.

He motioned for her to take a seat in the living room, where the faded, ragtag assortment of furniture had a scavenged look. She sat on a wooden straight-backed chair, reasoning it least likely to house fleas.

Daniel was staring at her with an expression of disbelief and warmth. "I can't believe you're here again."

"Yeah. It's kind of a surprise to me too. When I saw your email, I couldn't believe that Eva had shown up here. It seems too coincidental, you know?"

"Yes. I felt it too. I wondered if someone, or something, had driven her here."

Shiloh nodded. "When was she here?"

"Maybe a month ago?"

Shiloh's face fell. "Do you have any idea where she was headed?"

"She was looking for her father. I guess you know that."

"Yeah. I got that much."

Daniel kept staring. She felt the heat of the Hexcaliber and wondered if he had gained some sort of power, and if so, what.

But the confusion in his eyes didn't match up with the kind of piercing focus she had learned to recognize in people who had acquired magic power in one way or another. She was wondering where the Hex was picking up the magic signature in the air when a scalding jolt of heat caused her to grimace.

"Are you all right?" Daniel asked, as a woman slipped into the room behind him. Shiloh studied the woman, who was ordinary looking, perhaps in her 30s, with a kind of toughness about her face, as if she'd spent a lot of time working outdoors.

"Who have we here?" the woman asked, in a tone of unconvincing friendliness.

Shiloh met her eyes and immediately sensed the magic. Not a lot, but enough that the woman would be used to having things her way.

"This is Shiloh," said Daniel. He pointed at the woman and said, "Elvira."

Shiloh nodded, her eyes locked on the woman's.

"What brings you this way?" Elvira asked. As she spoke she stood behind Daniel and placed both her hands on his shoulders. Shiloh's gut clenched with distaste, but she tried not to let it show on her face.

"I'm looking for my daughter. Daniel saw her picture on a flyer and sent me an email. He thought maybe she had passed through here."

Elvira raised her eyebrows. "Did he now? Well, I hope he didn't get your hopes up over nothing. We see an awful lot of kids comin' through here. They's so many on the run these days. It's a shame."

Shiloh shifted her gaze to Daniel for a moment and saw conflict in his eyes, the anxious look of a person in chains. She looked back at Elvira's face, with its expression like that of a cat with a wounded bird in its claws.

"Yes," said Shiloh. "I'm really worried about my daughter. She's only thirteen. That's a dangerous age to be out on your own, especially now."

Elvira shook her head. Then she asked in a voice oozing with sympathy, "It's so hard with young girls. They all think they know more than they do."

Shiloh bit her tongue. "So, you don't remember seeing her?"

Elvira shook her head slowly. "It's hard to say. It might be that she was here, but they come and they go. If..."

"She took our horse," Daniel blurted.

Shiloh saw Elvira's grip tighten on his shoulders.

"Really? She's a good rider," Shiloh said.

Elvira frowned as if in thought and said, "Oh. Come to think, maybe I do recall that one. The girl who stole our horse. She wasn't here long. I don't suppose you could repay us for our horse?"

Shiloh gazed at her coolly. "Well, I'd be happy to pay for the horse if I were sure it was my daughter who took it. But you said you couldn't remember her."

A scowl flickered across Elvira's face, but she tried to cover it up with a smile. "Well, it's hard to remember every child who passes through. Horses are harder to come by."

Shiloh nodded. "Yeah. Times are tough all around." She stood up and, turning to Daniel, said, "Well, I've taken up enough of your time. Thanks for your help."

"Wait. Can't you stay for dinner? We don't have much, but we never turn anyone away."

Shiloh heard the plea in his voice. Elvira's mouth remained clamped shut in an approximation of a tight smile. Shiloh wondered what kind of punishment awaited Daniel after she left. She paused at the door and said, "I appreciate the offer, but I really can't stay. I need to find my daughter. But I'd be grateful for a bite to take with me, if that's not too much trouble." She spoke directly to Elvira, inflecting her voice with a layer of humility.

Elvira brightened and said, "Why sure, honey. I'll fix you a bag to go. I'll be right back." She shot a cautionary glance at Daniel before she left the room.

Shiloh knelt quickly beside Daniel and whispered, "Daniel, do you want to come with me? You don't have to stay here."

"I can't leave. She's counting on me. They all count on me."

"Oh yeah? Well who looks after you?"

"She does. She always helps me know what to do."

"I bet she does. Listen, I can't stay here now, but I can't leave you like this. Close your eyes for a second."

"Why?"

"Just do it, okay? I don't have time to explain, but I won't leave you defenseless. It's not right."

"What do you—"

He stopped as the sound of footsteps approaching reached them. Shiloh reached out and moved her palm across his face to shield his eyes while she cast a quick spell of protection over him. Then she stepped back just before Elvira entered carrying a cloth bag.

"Here you go. Some bread and cheese and apples. It's not much, but it's better than nothing," she said.

Shiloh took the bag. "Thanks," she said. She turned toward Daniel, who was staring at her, his eyes full of questions. She nodded at him and said, "Thanks, Daniel. Come see me if you ever get to Washington."

***

As she continued down the road, Shiloh wondered if she'd done enough to help Daniel. She owed him for helping her all those years ago. Seeing him under the thumb of that amateur witch left a bad taste in Shiloh's mouth. Which reminded her to toss the bag Elvira had given her into the bushes. Better to be safe than sorcered.

The warmth of the evening had given way to chilly dampness, and it was too dark to see where she was headed. A sensible person would conjure up a campfire and rest for the night, she told herself. But the sight of Daniel had stirred up a world of memories, and she was in no mood to think about roads not taken now. Her legs were tired, her stomach was empty, and she was starting to feel the pinch of fear. What if she never caught up with Eva? If she were on horseback she could be in Seattle by now.

Shiloh stood still and examined this thought. The trouble with remembering how it felt to be on the run was that she also remembered how reckless and foolish she'd been, when she was a young woman in her twenties. Eva was barely a teenager. What if...? A wave of nausea racked Shiloh as she contemplated some of the creepy possibilities waiting for a young girl alone in this broken world.

As she stared up at the stars, Shiloh remembered the argument she'd had with Josh just before she left, when he accused her of being stupid not to take advantage of Magda's magical tools for locating anyone or anything on Earth. All the air left her lungs as she suddenly felt the enormity of her pride and what it might have already cost her.

She shook herself and studied the Sourcer. The nearest vent looked to be a couple of miles away. She started jogging toward it.

CHAPTER 8

After a few wrong turns and missed signals, Shiloh stumbled through the murky mist into a clearing in sight of Magda's castle. She stared up at it with a shiver. She'd forgotten how immense it was.

It took her a while to reach the gate. She used the time rehearsing what she would say when she met the Dragon Queen again. Though Shiloh had communicated with her on an annual basis since she had taken the job of monitoring Earth's Deep Magic activity, she hadn't seen Magda face-to-face since they parted company in Seattle more than thirteen years ago. Shiloh wondered if the queen would look older, or if her magic kept her skin dewy fresh indefinitely.

At the gate Shiloh raised her hand to bang on the door. It swung open with a loud groan before she made contact. A lackey in leather and bronze gestured for her to enter.

"I'm here to see Magda," Shiloh offered.

"She's expecting you," said the lackey.

Shiloh shrugged. "Guess it'd be hard to throw a surprise party for her, huh?"

The lackey responded with, "Step this way," and walked toward the stone stairway carved into the wall of the castle's interior courtyard. Shiloh had a sudden flashback of running down that same stairway during her training period. So much had changed in her life since then, yet here it seemed time took the scenic route.

At the top of the stairs Shiloh turned to the lackey and said, "I think I can find my way from here."

"You are to follow me," the lackey said solemnly. He led her down a grand hallway she remembered perfectly. When they arrived at a massive double door carved with dueling dragons, the lackey bowed slightly and opened one of the doors for her. She went in and stopped cold.

The room was like nothing she'd seen before. Shimmering golden light streamed from a ceiling inset with a starburst pattern of enormous etched glass windows. Huge tapestries with unicorns and dragons wrought in silver thread lit the walls. The floor was a dazzling design in green and ivory marble. Magda's dragon motif throne was carved of dark wood that glowed like a living thing in the light that danced across the floor.

"Do you like it?" Magda smiled at her. "Some think it's gaudy, but I decided the old place needed a little more color. What do you think?"

"It's nice. Not exactly homey, but you probably weren't going for that."

Magda's smile widened. "This is what I've missed. No one around here would dare tell me that." She sighed happily. "So. What brings you here? Have you finished tidying up Jack's mess?"

"You know I haven't," Shiloh said. "You probably also know why I'm here, if I know you. And I do, so let's cut the crap. Where is she?"

"Where is who?"

"You know who."

"I assure you, I don't know what you're talking about. Last time I checked you were busy chasing some would-be wizard across the tundra."

"Don't bullshit me. I've been looking for my daughter for six months. You have that cauldron thingy. I'm asking for your help."

Magda raised her eyebrows and put the tips of her fingers together. "Six months! That's a long time, for someone with your skills. Perhaps your daughter doesn't want to be found."

Shiloh felt it then, even though the Hexcaliber was stone cold on her skin, she sensed the willful deceit that magic spawns, and saw the calculation behind Magda's cool mask.

"You know where she is," Shiloh said.

"Don't be absurd," Magda protested. "I have better things to do than mind other people's offspring. Perhaps if you'd been a better parent..."

"What do you know about being a parent? You and your kind—"

Just then the doors flew open and Eva burst into the room with a rainbow in her hands. "Look what I made..." she began. Then she saw Shiloh and stopped, the rainbow drooping in her hands.

"Eva, look who's come to visit!" Magda looked from mother to daughter and the amusement in her voice stoked the fury Shiloh had been keeping under control.

"I knew it!" she shrieked.

"Well if you did, I don't understand why you didn't come sooner," Magda purred.

"What is she doing here?" Eva whined, addressing Magda.

Magda shrugged. "I didn't invite her."

"You followed me here? Why did you bother?"

"Eva please! I've been worried sick about you. I've been looking everywhere."

"I'll bet. It's been six months. You couldn't have been looking too hard."

"Eva, I know I haven't been the best mother in the world but I love you. Let me take you home."

"Forget it! I'm never going back. This is my home now."

"But Eva —"

"I hate you. Don't you get it? You lied to me for years. I'll never trust you again. Never!"

"Please, Eva! I love you. You've got to believe me. I did what I thought was best."

Eva glared at Shiloh for a moment, then turned to Magda and said, "I'm sorry I interrupted. May I be excused?"

"Of course, dear. Run along."

"Wait! Where are you going? Can't we talk?" Shiloh implored.

Eva turned slightly at the door and addressed Shiloh in a tone of withering scorn. "What part of 'I hate you' don't you understand?"

She spun out of the room, unable to slam the doors because they weren't built for slamming, though when they did finish slowly closing, the resonant boom was thunderous as any operatic finale.

Magda sighed happily and sat back in her throne. "Teenagers are so dramatic. It's adorable, really," she said.

Shiloh glared at her. "You have no right to keep my daughter here for your own amusement."

"Oh really? I couldn't agree with you more. She eats a lot, too. Perhaps I should be asking you for room and board."

"You're insufferable, just like Jack!"

Magda's smile vanished. "You're in no position to dictate terms here. And rudeness will not serve you well when you're in my home."

"How did she get here? She couldn't have just stumbled in here. Do you deny that you had a hand in it?"

"Don't be absurd. If I'd wanted her I could have had her from the start. I respected your right as a mother. I would never have interfered."

"So how did she get here?"

"She's very bright." Magda's smile returned. "She came to me of her own free will. That's a human thing. You can't magic it away."

"Maybe so. But you could convince her to come back to Earth. Why won't you?"

"Why do you think? She's smart, young and gifted—a perfect protégée. She reminds me a little of you the way you used to be."

"Yeah, well, I've grown up."

"Unfortunately you've lost something in the process."

"My naiveté? Right. After thirteen years of stamping out magic fires, can you blame me if I'm a little burned out?"

"I don't blame you. But you shouldn't blame me for enjoying someone as fresh and high spirited as Evangeline. I may not live forever. Someone will have to rule after I'm gone. Why not her?"

"Because she doesn't belong here. She's human, for one thing."

"Oh please, you know that's not true. She's a hybrid—an improvement on the species. She has the potential to bring about a new Golden Age on Earth. You should be proud. Would you rather she were ordinary?"

"She's not yours," Shiloh growled.

"She's not yours either," Magda retorted.

"She's my daughter."

"She has Jack's genes. He hasn't figured that out yet, but wait a few years. Once she starts to flex her magic there will be no one—not you, certainly—who can stop her. That's why it's important that she get the right training. She must feel the truth within her. External laws are for those who lack judgment. Eva must embody wisdom. Do you really think you can teach her what she must know?"

"I don't trust you to do it," Shiloh said.

"I understand that. However, you really don't have any choice in this. Eva's not a little girl anymore. She's lost faith in you, and if you want her back you'll have to work. Frankly, if I were her I'd never believe you again."

"You could convince her to trust me."

"Why should I?"

"Because you owe me. I've given my whole life to fixing a problem that wasn't my fault. If anything, you and your whole wacky crew over here should have stepped up. But you couldn't be bothered."

Magda frowned ever so slightly. "I seem to recall that Rufio had a simple idea for eliminating the problem. You didn't care for it much."

"Are you serious? You honestly think wiping out all human life on Earth would have been fair?"

"I didn't say that. I'm merely pointing out that there were choices to be made, and you accepted the job that was offered. If you're not happy with the way things have worked out, we can revisit the decision. I believe Rufio would be more than happy to implement his idea."

Shiloh started pacing, her boots clacking on the smooth marble floor. "I suppose this is all entertaining for you. You think so little of humans. Yet, you know, you could pass for one."

Magda's expression darkened, but she recovered her poise almost immediately and replied, "Flawed as they are, humans still have many endearing qualities. It's a bit tedious watching them struggle against their own best interests, but I share your desire to save them from themselves. Ideally, magic could help humans grow spiritually and intellectually."

"How? As far as I can tell the only thing humans use magic for is to get power over each other. It's just another weapon."

"Ah, but unlike your primitive arsenal, magic also has the potential to heal, to inspire, to elevate and entertain. In the right hands magic can strip away the vanity and shortsightedness and replace it with the sense of awe and gratitude essential for a meaningful and productive life."

Shiloh sniffed derisively. "Yeah, sure. Who wouldn't want that? But the truth is you can't change humans with magic. No matter how long they live, they never grow up. They never stop fighting with each other."

"Ah, but you see in Theatros magic has been controlled for millennia and used to keep peace. Once we get the situation under control on Earth we anticipate similar results."

Shiloh shook her head impatiently. "Yeah, good luck with that. Anyway, this has nothing to do with Eva. She's my daughter. You have no right to take her from me."

"Fine. Take her back if you can."

Chapter 9

Shiloh stormed out of Magda's chamber without pausing to reflect that it was a big castle and she had no idea where Eva was. She stopped charging down the hall and stared out one of the windows overlooking the courtyard.

Memories of when she first came to Magda's fortress crowded into her mind's eye. How cocky and foolish she had been, convinced that she could overcome any obstacle to rescue her father. No wonder Eva was so reckless. No wonder Josh didn't think she was a good mother.

She leaned her head against the window and felt the weight of it all pressing down on her. She knew she hadn't been a good mother. But it was too much, trying to be a good parent while having to save the whole world from the dangerous power Jack had spread.

A flare of anger took the edge off her dark mood. She could blame Jack, she mused. But what good would that do? As her thoughts moved the chess pieces of the past around the board of the present, her eyes took in the scene below. Guards and serving staff went about their duties. A steady, unhurried dance of motion surrounded the central fountain, like a flower unfurling in slow motion. Shiloh wondered idly if that was how human activity appeared from a god's perspective. All well and good until someone tries to get a better view of the whole pageant. A god-like box seat. That was the seductive promise Deep Magic dangled in front of the restless souls who wanted more than mere ordinary life. God, if they only knew. She'd take ordinary life in a heartbeat if she could.

She sighed and turned away. It was way too late for that. If she'd never tried to find her father...the Earth would still be in danger, but she wouldn't be the only one responsible for keeping it safe.

A pair of Magda's palace guards appeared and quickly flanked her, demanding to know who she was and what business she had wandering around the Queen's private hall. When Shiloh told them she was Eva's mother, they seemed confused, until Shiloh added, "Listen, fellas, I'm not here to cause trouble. I just want to talk with my daughter. Can you tell me which room she's in?"

Shiloh figured it wouldn't hurt to play the ignorant female in a social system as backward as the Dragon Mountains'. She remembered what a stir her pants had caused years ago.

The guards insisted on clearing her story with Magda. After they were satisfied that Magda had no objection, they escorted Shiloh to a nearby corridor and left her at the door to Eva's room.

There, Shiloh hesitated. She couldn't remember the last time she'd actually sat down and talked with her daughter. In her mind's eye, Eva was still her little girl, wearing braids, skipping down the sidewalks of Georgetown, eating cupcakes. Innocent.

Shiloh closed her eyes and took a deep breath. The girl she'd just seen playing with a rainbow was someone else. But who?

She knocked gently on the door. There was no sound from inside, and for a moment Shiloh wondered if the guards had made a mistake. Then the door was yanked open and Eva's scowl hit her between the eyes.

"I knew it was you! Just the way you knocked. Even your knock is guilty," Eva said.

Shiloh blanched at the anger, but forced herself not to react. "Can I talk to you?"

"Does Magda know you're here?"

"She told me I could try to persuade you to come back home with me."

"Home? What's that? The place you never are? The place Josh lives? Is that your home? It isn't mine. This is where I live now."

"You don't belong here."

"You are so wrong. This is the first place I've ever felt like I belonged. Magda understands me. You don't even know me."

"I'm sorry my job has kept me away so much all these years. But I thought you were okay. I thought you were happy."

"Yeah? Well you were wrong. Why did you lie to me about my father? Magda told me he lives over here. But you never married him. Why?"

"It's complicated."

"That's not an answer. If that's the best you can do, just leave now. I've got nothing to say to you."

"Please." Shiloh looked deep into Eva's eyes, trying to catch a glimmer of warmth, but the girl's gaze was locked in contempt. "Can I just tell you my side of the story? Then if you don't want to come with me, I'll...I'll try to accept that."

Eva grimaced. "Fine," she snapped, stepping away from the door.

Shiloh barely glanced at the room, which looked much like the one she'd stayed in all those years ago, a stone-walled chamber softened with tapestries and rugs. The sole chair was currently occupied by a large black cat. Eva sat on the edge of the bed and fixed Shiloh with a cold stare. As Shiloh tried to figure out where to start, Eva folded her arms and swung her foot back and forth impatiently. "So...?" she said.

"Okay. I'm just not sure where to start. Do you want to know how I met him, or..."

Eva rolled her eyes. "It's your story. Just tell me the truth, the whole truth, and nothing but the truth." She smiled mockingly. "See? You can learn something from television."

Shiloh edged next to the cat, which hissed at her but didn't scratch. "All right, it began when my father disappeared—"

"Oh come on! I've met him. Don't mess with me or we're done."

Shiloh's air of eager pleading vanished. "I'm telling you what happened. My father vanished in the fall of my senior year in college. My mother told me he was dead."

Eva made a scoffing sound, but didn't interrupt.

"Yeah, sounds familiar to you I guess. But here's the difference: I was twenty-three. And I knew my father. And I knew something was wrong. So I left college and went to look for him. By myself. And, long story short, it turned out he'd been kidnapped by some tree-huggers in the backwoods outside of Seattle. They had...well...they had him locked in a place I couldn't get to unless I joined their group. So I did. And that's how I met your father."

"He was one of them?"

"Yes. But it turned out that they weren't as smart as they thought, and the whole time they were trying to bring the forestry industry to its knees, there were these other people...well, just one crazy person really...who wanted to reverse the industrial revolution...to put the genie back in the bottle. You understand? And when that happened—"

"Wait a minute. What about my father?"

"I'm getting to that. When the Greening happened the whole world changed really fast. You probably learned about it in school..."

"Yeah, sure. Terrorists destroyed the infrastructure, blah, blah. What has this got to do with my father? Was he a good guy or a bad guy?"

Shiloh took a deep breath. She hadn't told anyone the whole story in so long, she was surprised how it still affected her, how easily she could remember the way the light fell on Forest's face.

"He was... Well, at first I wasn't sure. I thought he was bad, because of what they did to my dad. But then later he helped me rescue my dad, and... Well, I guess we fell in love, for a while, and I wasn't sure where I was supposed to be or how I should live my life, but then I... I was put in charge of a very important mission on Earth, and I didn't want your father to give up his life here for that."

"What do you mean? How could you be put in charge of anything? You're like the least responsible person I know. You can't even cook."

"Yeah, I know. Bad mom. You said that. But there were things I learned while I was here—"

"Wait! Wait. When were you here? How were you here? Did you go through the vent thing?"

"Yes. I was here before you were born. With your father. And I met Magda. She taught me some things, and... She asked me to take the job on Earth. So I did." Shiloh stopped, wondering how much she had to tell Eva. The whole truth wouldn't be easy to swallow.

"Did you love my dad?"

"For a while, yes."

"But you left him? Before I was born?"

"Yes."

"And he never knew I existed until... How did he find out about me? He must have found out, because he wrote that letter."

"I don't know." She pursed her lips and considered how much she could reveal without making things worse. "Someone over here must have let it slip."

Eva stared at her for a few moments in silence. "Were you ever going to tell me about him?"

Shiloh shrugged. "I didn't think it would help."

Eva jumped up and screamed, "Well you were wrong! It would have helped a lot! Just to know I had a father. To even know his name. What he looked like. Where he came from. You had no right to keep it from me!"

Shiloh stood up and reached for her, saying, "I know, I know. I'm so sorry—"

"Stop saying that. I don't care how sorry you are. It doesn't change anything. I'll hate you forever for what you did.

And if you think I'm ever letting you back in my life you can forget it. But..." She paused and sat back down. "Where is he?"

"Your father?"

Eva answered with a glare of such burning fury that Shiloh stepped back before she replied, "I don't know. I have an idea. I could probably find him."

"Probably? That's the best you can do?"

Shiloh sighed. "It's been thirteen years. He could have moved."

Eva looked at her with stony contempt. Then she said, "Here's the deal: you take me to him. If that goes well..."

Shiloh waited for the conclusion. When it appeared Eva didn't have a plan for how to finish that sentence Shiloh said, "Okay. Let's say I take you to him, assuming I can find him. If, after meeting him and talking to him you still want to hate me, that's your choice, but I would like you to agree to come back to Earth, to see your grandfather one last time. He's old, you know, and he's all alone. And he loves you." She hesitated before adding, "My parents knew about your father. They never blamed me for leaving him."

"Huh. So they were in on it." She shook her head and glared. "Fine. Maybe grandpa will tell me something you won't. If you take me to my father, and if that goes well, I'll go back to visit grandpa. But I'm not going back to D.C. with you. That's never gonna happen."

"Josh misses you."

Eva frowned. "Sorry. He's part of your thing. I can't be around that anymore."

Shiloh stood for a moment, dazed and disoriented as if she'd been in a car crash and managed to walk away from the wreckage. "Okay," she said, quietly.

At the door she turned her head, but Eva refused to look at her.

***

Alone in her room, Eva picked up the black cat and stroked it while she considered her situation. Her mother was a bore. She'd never realized it before, but in the last few months she was seeing things differently. Most adults were so pathetically needy. It was almost comical, really, when she thought back to her childhood—how much she'd longed for her mother's approval. Eager to show her every new skill, to show her drawings, tell her about her adventures, ask questions. But with her mother gone so much of the time, Eva had learned to figure things out on her own. She'd learned that adults couldn't tell the difference between a lie and a truth. And she'd decided that adults, for the most part, weren't worth the trouble. In fact, as Eva tickled the cat under its chin and listened to its soft purr, she wasn't sure what to do with the new skills that she'd been gaining. The cat, for instance. Formerly a velvet pillow, the cat had morphed into existence at Eva's whim. She hadn't even tried to make it happen. One minute she was wishing she had a cat, and the next minute Tremelo was there, rubbing against her leg.

Magda had explained that such magic was easier to work in Dragonmere, because it was built upon a bedrock of Deep Magic. She also had told Eva that transmutive effects such as animation of the inanimate were nearly impossible on Earth. By now Eva had heard enough lies from adults that she could detect the false note of a half-truth.

She snorted softly as she set the cat down on the stone floor and stood up. She walked over to the window and gazed out at the deep purple shadows in the mountain clefts. Somewhere in this world her father lived. Was he another liar? She sighed impatiently. She would humor her mother long enough to find out. But after that...? Well, it might be time to take this magic growing in her bones for a test drive and see how far she could go.

CHAPTER 10

"Do you even know where you're going?"

The petulant tone of Eva's voice was like sand in a shoe. Shiloh would have stopped to shake it out, but she was fearful of losing her cool completely and shouting at her daughter. Probably not a smart move, considering the glimpses she'd had of Eva's emerging magic chops. The kid didn't know her own strength, that was for sure.

Shiloh held her tongue and continued thrashing through the dangling vines and trip-worthy roots snarling the uphill path. The first portion of their journey had been smooth to the point of boredom, thanks to Magda providing them with a dragon escort through the tunnels under her domain and the Red Plains. They had been on foot ever since their arrival at the border of the Green Wood.

Shiloh didn't remember much about the route from Jack's tree castle to the tunnel entrance, except that it had been all downhill before. Now the slick, overgrown path was more treacherous. Eva's caustic remarks didn't help.

When they finally emerged onto a small grassy clearing, Shiloh felt a twinge of memory. The path leveled out. Soon they entered another forest of taller trees, where birdsong and insect buzz filled the air.

"I don't understand why you can't just magic us there," whined Eva.

Shiloh paused, reined in her impatience, and repeated the explanation she'd offered before they started. "I don't know where your father is. To find out we have to see Jack. Even if he knows, he may not be willing to tell us right away." She pursed her lips, noting how Eva's shirt was clinging to her sweaty torso. She was no little girl anymore. Shiloh stifled her objections to everything about this mission. There was nothing to be gained by going over it anymore. She just had to face down Jack and keep Eva from talking too much.

"Who is this guy Jack, anyway?" Eva asked.

"He's the boss around here. He was Forest's boss."

"Huh." Eva stared at her without a hint of emotion. "Forest what?"

"What do you mean?"

"I mean, Forest Jones? Forest Tree? What's his last name?"

"Oh. I don't think he has one." Shiloh shrugged. "I never thought about it."

"Some responsible adult you are."

"Hey. I was going through a lot when I met him."

Eva shook her head and said, "You're pathetic."

Shiloh turned away and resumed walking. Soon enough she'd have to tango with Jack. She wasn't going to waste comeback lines in an argument she couldn't win.

When they came out of the woods into the broad clearing surrounding Jack's dwelling, she stopped to allow Eva to take it in. Shiloh remembered vividly her first glimpse of the extraordinary, living castle. The tree rose high above the forest, with branches and turrets extending far and wide. Golden light spilled from mullioned windows, smoke drifted from crooked chimneys, moss grew everywhere. Shiloh glanced at Eva to see her reaction, but the teenager was maintaining her bored stiff facade. Whether or not it was genuine only she knew.

Shiloh shook her head and headed to the doors. The elves guarding the entrance bowed to her, which came as a surprise. She said, "I'm Shiloh Carter. I'm here to see Jack."

The elves nodded and opened the gate without hesitation. Shiloh realized that Jack probably had been watching her since she set foot in the Green Wood. She'd have to step more carefully. If he'd been watching, he'd also have heard everything she said. She glanced back at Eva, who was smirking at her.

They entered the castle and Shiloh heard Eva whisper, "Wow."

Shiloh allowed herself a small smile. *Yeah, kid. That's more like it.*

A young female elf stepped forward and said, "Welcome. You wish to have an audience with the King. Please follow me."

As they followed the small elf girl up the curving staircase, Eva tugged on Shiloh's sleeve and said in an undertone, "He's a king?"

"He can call himself anything he wants. It's his castle. He'll always be Jack to me."

They were led to a tall carved doorway that looked familiar to Shiloh. The elf guards seated on stools at either side of the door looked exactly as they had when she'd seen them last. "Hello boys. I'm here to see Jack," she said.

"We know. He knows," they said in unison, their voices buzzing like pencil sharpeners. They stared at Eva. She stared back and stuck her tongue out at them as she passed by. Shiloh heard the elves giggling as the door closed.

The room opened out into a balustraded balcony overlooking the forest. Jack was standing at the railing with his back to them, but he turned at the sound of the door closing and smiled.

"Shiloh. How good of you to come and visit an old man."

"You're no man," she said. "And I'm not that good."

Jack's grin widened. "You haven't changed a bit. But this young lady has," he said, staring at Eva. He glided across the room with his arms held out as if he expected a hug. Eva glared and folded her arms across her chest.

"Ah. She's just like you," Jack said, clasping his hands together in front of him as if he were a benevolent innkeeper.

"Yeah. Well. I'm hoping she'll be a little smarter than I was," Shiloh said.

"Oh, don't be so hard on yourself. You did pretty well for a human. But this child..." Jack paused to allow himself a smile blended in equal parts of glee and gloat. Then he lifted his head and asked brightly, "So! What brings you here?"

Shiloh sighed impatiently. "Do we really have to do this, Jack? I think you know why I'm here. Why *we're* here. Eva wants to meet her father, and I promised I would help her do that."

"Perfectly understandable." Jack beamed innocently and waited.

"Oh come on, Jack. I know he's living with Lyra, but I don't know where."

"Oh. I see. So you didn't come to visit a lonely old king and brighten his dinner table with lively conversation?"

Shiloh stole a glance at Eva and was dismayed to see that she was grinning. *Damned elvish charm.* It didn't help matters that Jack's magic allowed him to appear as handsome as he chose, and in his castle he pulled out all the stops.

"Well, I was hoping we could just get going," she said, "seeing as how, you know, I have that job back on Earth, and there's no one else going to do it."

"Oh that shouldn't be a problem. I can always send someone there to take over for you. If you're getting worn out by it all. I wouldn't blame you. Such a nuisance. And I'm sure you'd like to spend more time with your daughter."

"Hey! I'm right here. And I don't want to spend more time with her. I just want to meet my dad, okay? But..." Eva shot a glance at Shiloh before she continued, "I've waited this long. I wouldn't mind some food."

"No!" Shiloh glared at Eva, and then turned it on Jack. "I know what you're trying to do. And so help me, I'll fight you as long as I live. You already ruined my life. I'm not going to let you ruin hers."

Jack held up his hands in protest. "Please, my dear. Calm yourself. I'm not a monster. I'm not going to take your firstborn child. Although..." he leveled his green gaze at her and smiled wickedly, "we both know I could."

He sighed happily and winked at Eva. "Don't worry. Your mother and I would never do anything to hurt you."

He strolled over to the balcony. "You know, I think it would be good for Eva to learn a little bit about our world. After all, it could be hers someday."

"Jack. Give it up. If you won't help us, we'll find Forest on our own."

"Oh I don't think so. In fact, I can guarantee you won't find Miss Lyra unless you stay for dinner with me. That's not asking too much." He glanced at Eva and added, "And Eva's hungry. Do it for her sake."

Shiloh rolled her eyes, but Eva said, "Come on, Mom. I'm starving and my feet hurt. Let's just stay here tonight, and we can go see my dad in the morning."

Shiloh shook her head. But the truth was, she was hungry and tired also. The day was almost over. "Okay. You win. But just tonight. That's it. In the morning we leave. And you help us find Lyra."

Jack smiled easily. A little too easily, Shiloh thought.

***

As the last bite of sumptuous pie was sliding down her throat Shiloh nearly choked at the sound of Eva giggling at another one of Jack's jokes. His humor nearly always hinged on his notions of the inadequacy of other species. It reminded Shiloh all too vividly of the sort of racist humor she'd heard when she was growing up. She would have preferred to leave the table, but she wasn't going to leave Eva alone with Jack, and she didn't want to provoke another argument in front of him. As she searched for some way to change the subject she noticed a small crystal unicorn sculpture on the mantel, and suddenly she recalled Jessie, the gypsy wanna-be from North Carolina Jack had allowed into Theatros back when Shiloh was going home.

"Say, Jack, what ever became of Jessie?" she asked.

His expression turned to one of distaste. "Ahem. That experiment was not a success," he said, with the air of someone who doesn't want to discuss it.

Perfect. "Really? She seemed so eager to learn, and so enthusiastic about coming here. What happened? I thought for sure you two kids would hit it off."

Jack flared his nostrils at her. "Oh, did you? Or did you think she would be so annoying that she would keep me too busy to regret letting you go?"

"You didn't let me go. I left. Period."

Jack shrugged. "The point is not worth disputing. The fact remains that, while superficially she has a certain appeal, she lacks the intellectual quality that I require in a consort."

"I thought you just wanted a plaything."

"Toys lose their charm. One grows weary of simplicity. I needed a new challenge. And I could see she wasn't happy here."

"So what happened to her?"

"As it turned out I had been looking for a way to get back at Rufio for some ill-considered remarks he's made over the years, and it seemed like a perfect opportunity."

"You sent her to Rufio? That crazy barbarian?"

Jack smiled. "It was one of my more inspired ideas. Miss Jessie had never warmed to my sophisticated style. She accused me of..." he hesitated, "well, let's just say we were incompatible. Her so-called romantic ideas were so hackneyed and tedious. I introduced her to Rufio and she lit up like a sprite on Midsummer's Eve."

Shiloh laughed. "I guess that's all right then. But what about Rufio? He didn't seem like the romantic type to me."

"Wait," Eva said. "I met a guy named Rufio when I first got here. Big guy, mostly naked?"

Shiloh stared at her. "When did you meet Rufio? How?"

"I just ran into him when I was looking for Dad. He loaned me a horse."

Shiloh looked at Jack. "Did you arrange that?"

"No. I'm as surprised as you are," he said dryly.

Shiloh turned to Eva. "I can't believe he loaned you a horse."

"I know," said Jack. "He's not a giver."

"He seemed okay to me," Eva said, with a complacent shrug.

Shiloh stared at her, unable to decipher whether her daughter was trying to upset her on purpose or simply doing it without trying.

"Well, that's interesting," Jack said. "Perhaps Jessie's a calming influence on the Red Ruler."

"Huh. Maybe. Maybe she's been getting him stoned," Shiloh said, and immediately regretted it as she saw Eva's eyes glitter with interest.

"Oh you knew about that, did you?" Jack asked.

"I knew she wanted to bring her "special" stash here. I told her she shouldn't bother. Maybe she didn't listen to me."

Eva was grinning. "I'll have to meet her," she said.

"I don't think so," said Shiloh, grimly.

"Now, now, we mustn't rush to judgment. I knew of the girl's...ahem... horticultural hobby, but I never imagined she'd find a willing sponsor in Rufio, of all creatures. My, my. Perhaps I underestimated the little vixen."

"She wasn't stupid," said Shiloh. "She just seemed a little inexperienced and naive."

Jack shrugged. "Well, she's all grown up now, and if she's tamed that hot-headed savage, it works for me. It's like that old human saying, taking care of two birds with one stoned."

Shiloh resisted the urge to smile, knowing it would only encourage him. Jack took advantage of the moment anyway, turning his focus to Eva.

"Well my dear, you've certainly grown up in a hurry. The last time I saw your mother you were just a little secret she was carrying around inside. Now here you are."

Eva leaned back in her chair, watching him the way a deer watches a hunter.

Shiloh tried to think of something to deflect Jack's interest, but she realized the inquiry was inevitable. Better it should happen while she was there to witness.

"There's something that's been puzzling me, Eva," Jack began. "In all the hundreds of years I've lived here, no human has ever stumbled through a vent by accident and lived to tell the tale. Yet here you are. Why do you suppose that is?"

"How would I know?" Eva said. "Maybe I'm the chosen one."

Jack grinned. "My thought exactly. I think you're here for a reason. And it's not simply to meet your Daddy."

"And why do you think I'm here?"

"I think you belong here."

"Huh. You don't know me."

"Perhaps not. But I may understand you better than you think."

"Well, join the club!" Eva blurted, flinging a hand toward Shiloh. "You and Magda and every old fart I've met since I left D.C. They all wanna tell me where I belong, what I should do, blah, blah, blah. Get over yourselves. You may be the boss around here, but you're not the boss of me. Nobody is. And nobody's gonna be. The only reason I came here was to meet my dad, and I'm starting to think he's probably gonna turn out to be just like the rest of you. Full of worthless advice."

"My, my. Aren't we the little rebel without a pause?" Jack made no effort to hide his amused smile, and its effect on Eva was like gas on a tire fire.

"Let's get out of here," she snapped, looking at Shiloh.

Shiloh said, "You're forgetting one thing. He knows where Forest is. We don't."

Eva glowered at Jack.

Shiloh took a deep breath, let it out, and said, "Okay. It's been a long day. Maybe we should get some sleep and finish this in the morning." She stared pointedly at Jack.

He nodded to her and said, "Certainly. Mitra will show you to your rooms."

A slender, dark-eyed elf girl appeared from the shadows. They followed her through a twisting moss-carpeted hall lit with twinkling golden lights suspended from the ceiling. The air smelled of damp earth and ferns.

Shiloh had been hoping they would share a room, though she realized that was the last thing Eva wanted at this point. Eva had been reluctant even to make eye contact during the trip so far.

Alone in her room, Shiloh was assailed with unexpected memories of the first time she came to Jack's. So much younger, so much less experienced. She thought of Eva and how this whole new world must look to her young eyes. But as she tried to put herself in Eva's head, Shiloh was struck by how little she knew of Eva's actual feelings. She'd never had the luxury of time to spend with her own daughter. Not to mention that the world in which Eva had grown up was so radically different from the complacent, consumer-centric bubble Shiloh had known as a child. In the post-Greening world, nothing material could be taken for granted, and the assumptions of the spiritual support systems had been fractured and warped to such an extent that consensus was almost non-existent.

No wonder Eva was such a cynic. It made Shiloh sad, but as she lay down and watched the twinkling glow-lights in the ceiling, she was too tired to weep.

CHAPTER 11

Eva seemed in good spirits the next morning when Shiloh found her sampling another lavish spread in Jack's dining room. Shiloh resisted the urge to say something bright and cheerful to her. No sense ruining her daughter's good mood first thing.

They ate in silence. Eva acted as if Shiloh weren't there, until she'd finished eating. Then she stood up from the table and looked around the room before finally sighing and turning to Shiloh, who was draining a cup of something that came close, but not close enough, to being coffee.

"Are you ready to go?" Eva asked.

"Sure," Shiloh said, putting down the unfinished cup of brown fluid.

An elf girl met them at the door and told them Jack was waiting in the garden. Shiloh growled under her breath. Eva went skipping ahead of their elf guide.

The smile Jack wore as they came into view set alarm bells ringing in Shiloh's mind. The Jack she remembered didn't get that much pleasure out of making other people happy.

"Good morning. I trust you slept well," he said, gesturing toward another bench.

"Yeah. It was great, thanks. Now how do we get to Forest's house?" Shiloh asked, hoping to avoid another verbal duel with the old fox.

"Aah," Jack replied, and the sudden shift in his expression made the faux-coffee in Shiloh's stomach curdle. "I'm afraid I have some good news and some bad news."

Eva frowned. "What? What's the bad news?"

"Wouldn't you like the good news first?" Jack asked.

Shiloh shook her head. "If this is your idea of a joke, Jack, it's not even close to funny. Where's Forest?"

"Ah, well, it appears I may have misled you when I said he was at Lyra's. I sent someone to check on him last night after you left, and it seems he's no longer living there. Lyra and the three children are still there. But I'm told she has no idea where he went."

"What?" Eva shrieked.

"Three children?" Shiloh said.

"Yes. I thought they only had two. Apparently The Forester hasn't lost his touch," Jack said.

Shiloh sank onto the other garden bench. Eva remained on her feet, rocking back and forth like a fighter waiting for the bell.

"And you don't know where he is? I thought you were supposed to be the big know-it-all around here. How can you be so clueless?" Eva demanded.

Shiloh turned to Jack and said, "Are you sure you can't tell us where he is? What did Lyra say?"

"She wasn't forthcoming. It's possible she thought I wanted to make him do something for me. She might have been lying about him being gone. It's not likely. Lyra's loyal to me. But it's conceivable he's still there. I certainly don't know."

"Well you should. What kind of ruler are you?" Eva stared at Jack with all the scorn at her disposal, which was a lot.

Shiloh sighed, looking at Jack. "Lyra wouldn't lie. Not even to protect Forest. She loves him, but she cares about you, too. God knows why."

She stood up and said, "I want to see Lyra. Will you at least help us get to her place?"

"Certainly. You want to leave immediately, I take it?"

Shiloh and Eva said "Yes" in unison, then looked at each other in a flash of surprised solidarity.

Jack gestured to one of his guards, and within minutes Shiloh and Eva were seated on a sleek barge that moved silently without any visible means of power across the silvery lake surrounding Jack's mist-shrouded island.

Shiloh wished she could have a talk with Eva before they arrived at Lyra's, but their elf escorts had the keen ears of their kind, and no doubt anything they heard would be reported to Jack, if he wasn't already listening in.

When they reached the shore, the elves led them along a narrow trail winding through a dense forest of tall birch-like trees. Several times Shiloh thought she saw faces peering at them from behind the trees. She was glad for the elf escort then. Her memories of a narrow escape from a feral elf years ago remained vivid.

They emerged into a broad clearing that ended at a bluff overlooking a small valley. A tiny village lay at the center. Vineyards and small farms clung to the foothills of the surrounding mountains.

The elf escorts told Shiloh they would wait on the bluff while she and Eva went down to see Lyra. They pointed out a cottage at the far end of the village and watched as Shiloh and Eva started down the hillside.

As they tramped down the goat trail through knee-high rough grass, Eva broke the silence. "Do you really think he'll be there or were you just trying to get away from Jack?"

"I don't know. He might be there. Jack's such a liar. The only way to know is to see for ourselves."

"Why would he lie about my dad?"

"They kind of had a falling out. Forest used to work for Jack. But he had a change of heart and... It's a long story."

"Are you ever going to tell me the whole truth?"

"I'm telling you the truth now. Forest once tried to overthrow Jack. And Jack never forgave him for that."

"Really? No shit? So my dad's a badass?"

Shiloh stopped and turned to face Eva. "Not really—well... A little. He's a good man. He was always trying to do the right thing. It's just...it's not always easy to know what that is. Your dad was mixed up with some bad people when I met him. Things got complicated."

"But why did Dad want to overthrow Jack anyway?"

Shiloh tried to think of some way to tell the truth without telling all of it. "Well, for one thing, Jack was... interested in me at that time."

"Get out! Why you?" Eva gaped at her.

"You may find this hard to believe but I was considered reasonably good-looking when I was younger."

"Oh, shut up. You're still hot and you know it. But if Jack's got all this power and stuff, why would he want you? Couldn't he have anyone he wanted?"

"Maybe. I don't know really know. It had something to do with the fact that he wanted to have a kid, and apparently it's not easy to keep kids alive over here. The elves have brought humans over here for breeding purposes for centuries, because humans are more fertile or something. That's what he told me, anyway."

Eva made no attempt to feign indifference to this bit of family history. "I can't believe the king of the elves hit on you," she said.

"Yeah, well. Forest didn't like it much."

"I guess not. But I still don't get it. Jack's pretty hot too. But you turned him down, I'm assuming."

"Jack is Jack. He's not someone I trust."

Eva snorted disdainfully. "He's a king. Who cares if you can trust him?" She started down the path but Shiloh grabbed her wrist and pulled her back.

"Don't be a fool," she said. "Jack might seem like a fun guy to you, but I've seen him kill someone with a snap of his fingers. And it didn't mean anything to him. He's a powerful, crazy guy who's used to getting things his way. You do *not* want to mess with him."

Eva yanked her arm free and scowled at Shiloh. "You don't know what I want."

She turned and hurried down the hill. Shiloh squinted up at a hawk circling high above the valley; then she lowered her chin and followed her light-footed daughter.

When Lyra opened the door she hugged Shiloh without a word, then turned to look at Eva. "You must be—"

"Eva, the daughter," Eva said in a surly tone.

"Yes," Lyra said, gazing at her. "Please come in."

The kitchen dominated the space inside the cottage. Two children were playing in front of a fireplace. Babbling sounds issued from a cradle near the window. Herbs hung from exposed beams in the low ceiling.

"Would you like some tea?" Lyra asked.

"No thanks. We don't really have time for a visit. I think you know why we're here," Shiloh said.

Lyra nodded. "Jack's guards told me you are looking for Forest. I wish I could help you."

"So he's really not here?" Eva asked.

Lyra's eyes darted to Eva's face again. She shook her head slowly. "You look..." she began, then faltered and closed her eyes for a second.

"Are you all right?" Shiloh asked.

Lyra nodded quickly. She lifted her chin and said, "I'm sorry. It's just...when I look at Eva I see him. In her eyes. The bones of her face. And you too, of course. It's just...a bit...I'll be fine."

Shiloh shook her head. "I'm sorry to intrude. We didn't mean to upset you."

Lyra managed a small smile. "No. It's fine. You're a beautiful girl," she said to Eva. "I'm glad to meet you."

Eva glanced around the room with an air of restless boredom. "Do you have any idea where my dad is?" she asked.

"Yes. He went back to Earth to look for you."

"What?" Eva said.

"When did he leave?" Shiloh asked.

"It was almost a month ago." Lyra hesitated a few seconds. "I told him to go."

"What?" Shiloh said. "Why?"

"Please sit down," Lyra said. "I have to take care of Jasper." She went to the cradle and lifted the baby, whose coos had turned to cries. These stopped as soon as Lyra held him. She sat down in a rocking chair and lifted her shirt. The baby eagerly latched on to her breast, and the room became quiet.

"He wanted me to believe he was happy here. He seemed all right when he was with the children. But I saw the sadness. It never left him. He was trying to forget you, but you were still in his heart. It was only natural. I knew he didn't love me. I hoped he might come to feel something. He was always kind. But..." She sighed and shrugged her shoulders carefully, not to disturb the baby.

"When did he find out about me?" Eva asked.

"Nine years ago. One day Jack asked him to take care of some problem over in the Green Wood. There wasn't a problem. Jack was bored. He'd gotten rid of that girl by then. And he'd been watching you ever since you left. You know about that?"

"I guessed as much," Shiloh said.

"Jack knew you had given birth to Forest's child, and he loves secrets. But he loves telling them even more." She paused and looked at Eva. "He told Forest about you."

Lyra shifted the baby to her other breast. "When he came home that day I knew something had changed. He was restless and short with the children. He couldn't sleep. Finally he told me what had happened. He was heartsick and troubled with guilt. He wanted to go see you then. I encouraged him to write first. I was afraid he might upset your life." She bit her lip. "And I was afraid he would leave me."

Shiloh nodded. "It's okay. I understand."

"He sent a letter to your parents' house. You never replied. Jack told him you had received the letter. So he thought that you must be angry with him, or that you never wanted to see him again. Or both." She gently lifted the sleeping baby to lean upon her shoulder while she rocked in the chair.

"Years passed and I hoped he had accepted it. But the sadness grew inside him. You could see it in his face. He hardly ever smiled. He was losing his battle with sorrow. So... I told him to go find you."

Shiloh muttered, "Hell."

Eva stood up. "Okay. So this means we go back to D.C.?"

Shiloh sighed and stood up. "I guess. He's probably not there now."

"But he could be," Eva said.

Shiloh turned to Lyra. "Thank you. I'm sorry about everything."

"I know. It's not your fault. We cannot choose who we love."

"You deserve his love," Shiloh said. "I never did."

"Don't say that. And it is of no matter. My children give me all the love I could ask for. I am happy here."

Shiloh could see through the veil Lyra drew over her own suffering, but she knew better than to call her on it. She hugged the elf woman and kissed the baby as she said goodbye.

Eva left without a backward glance.

As they trekked back up the hill to the spot where Jack's guards waited, Shiloh said, "You were rude to Lyra."

"So?"

Shiloh stopped walking. "So? So that's not how you treat someone who tries to help you."

"She didn't help me. She just wants him back. She couldn't care less about me."

"What is wrong with you?"

"Nothing. I'm great. I'm better than great. It's all you so-called grown-ups that are broken. 'Wah, wah, my boyfriend doesn't love me.' No man is ever going to break my heart, I can tell you that."

"You say that now. Wait till you fall in love."

"I'm not planning on it."

"No one plans on it. It just happens."

"Like it happened to you?"

Shiloh felt the sting of scorn in Eva's voice. She fought to control her temper. The kid was only thirteen, after all. She took a deep breath and tried again.

"I'm just saying things happen in life. And sometimes innocent people get hurt through no fault of their own. Lyra is good person. Forest should have been happy with her."

"Oh really? And how come you weren't happy with him? And why didn't you tell him about me? Or were you planning to get rid of me?"

"How can you say that? I love you, even if you are..."

"Go on. Say it. A little bitch? A selfish brat?"

"You're a wonderful girl. But you do have things to learn about how to treat people."

"Oh really? Like you're such a great example."

"I haven't been perfect, but I've had a lot on my plate. You don't know—"

"So tell me! Tell me the whole truth for once! Why did you leave my father? Why were you never around when I was little, when I needed you? Why does everyone over here want a piece of me? Is it because I'm your kid? What's so special about you? It can't be because of my dad. Lyra's kids are related to me, right? I've got little elf stepbrothers. But nobody cares about them. So what's the deal?"

Shiloh glanced up at the top of the hill where the guards were watching them. And possibly listening in.

"Okay," she said, lowering her voice. "Sit down.

"The reason I wasn't around for you when you were little is...okay, I have to back up here a little bit. Don't roll your eyes at me. You asked for this. So, when my dad disappeared—"

"Oh please. How many times do I have to hear this sob story?"

"Do you want to know why you're so special or not?"

Eva bristled but said, "I'm listening."

"I'll make this short. Back in the last century Jack didn't like the way things were going on Earth. Too many people, too many trees being cut down, forests destroyed, et cetera. You must have learned about this in school."

"Sure. What does it have to do with me?"

"You know your grandfather was in the lumber business. That's why the Radicals kidnapped him and grafted him into a tree."

"They what, now?"

"They strapped him to a tree and used magic to lock him inside the tree."

Eva scowled and started to stand up. "If you're just going to bullshit me you can save your breath."

"It's the truth. I didn't believe it either, at first. And they, the Radicals, they didn't understand that they were being used by Jack. It was all Jack's doing, the whole thing. He tricked them all into believing they were part of some kind of revolutionary movement, when really the whole reason Jack got involved was that he didn't want humans messing up his playground."

Eva let out a loud sigh. "I thought you were going to give me the short version."

"Fine," Shiloh said, glancing up at the guards. "To make a long story short, when I found out what they'd done to my dad I made a deal with Jack that I would take the job of monitoring Deep Magic on Earth, to make sure humans didn't learn how to use it, and in return Jack gave me a tattoo that enabled me to undo the magic process that had locked my dad inside the tree."

"So? You're special because you have a tattoo? Everybody I know has a tattoo."

"Not like mine. Jack gave it to me himself, and he didn't use a needle. I didn't realize it at the time, but that tattoo injected Deep Magic inside me. Where you were at the time." Shiloh paused, watching Eva.

Eva stared at her sullenly for a few seconds. "Soooo...you're saying I have Deep Magic in me?"

"I'm afraid so."

"Huh. Well that explains a lot." Eva stared at her mother for a long minute. "So, that's why you were gone all the time when I was growing up? You were out undoing magic?"

"Pretty much."

"Huh. I guess that's not as lame an excuse as it could be." She glanced up at the guards. "Do they know you can do magic?"

"Maybe. Over here it's not so uncommon. Why do you ask?"

"I was just thinking, why should we take orders from Jack if you've got power too?"

"My power is nothing like Jack's. He's the real deal. He's been around for centuries and you don't last that long by playing nice."

Eva nodded. "So, he's kind of like my uncle. My magic uncle."

Shiloh raised her eyebrows. "I guess you could look at it that way. But you don't want to get too close to him."

"Why not? He could teach me some cool stuff, I bet."

Shiloh shook her head. "You don't belong over here. You're a human girl. You should be back on Earth with your own kind."

"But you just admitted it: I'm not like anyone else. I've got Deep Magic inside me. And not like you. I was born with it. That makes me super special. No wonder Jack wants me around."

Shiloh frowned at her. "I thought you wanted to meet your father. You could learn something from him."

Eva shrugged. "I'm not so sure about that anymore. I guess I'd still like to meet him. Although he couldn't be that hot if you left him, right?"

"I left him to take care of Earth. Somebody had to go, and Jack wasn't going to let Forest live unless he stayed here with Lyra. That was the deal."

"And you're saying you never loved my dad?"

"I did love him for a while, but not as much as he wanted me to. Besides, I felt responsible for The Greening. I couldn't just abandon Earth. I wanted to go back and try to help."

"Why? They had it coming. All those greedy fools with their SUVs and big TVs. Why should you help them?"

Shiloh stared at Eva, trying in vain to see some grain of compassion in her daughter's face. As a mother, she wanted to believe her daughter would outgrow adolescent self-centeredness. But she worried that along with the magic in her blood Eva may have inherited some of Jack's cold disdain for humanity.

Shiloh stood up and said, "Come on. We've spent enough time here."

Eva remained sitting in the tall grass. "I'm not going back," she announced.

"What do you mean?"

"I mean I like it here. I've changed my mind about meeting my father. It sounds to me like he was a wimp anyway. Compared to Jack." She grinned as she said this, and Shiloh nearly lost it.

"Oh yeah? So what about all that grief about how I'm such a liar and never told you the truth? Now I've told you and you've changed your mind?"

"Why should you care?"

"I care because I'm your mother and I've loved you since before you were born, and I'm not going to let you make the same mistakes I made."

"You don't get to pick my mistakes."

Shiloh's lungs collapsed. She struggled to catch her breath, choking on her rage. "Listen. I know you're not me. I know the world you've grown up in is so different from the one I knew that we may never understand each other. And I get that you hate me now. I probably would have hated my mother if she'd treated me the way I've treated you. So I'm not going to ask you to stay with me, or even come back to Earth to stay. All I'm asking is that you follow through on the mission we started out with. To meet your father. I think he deserves that much. And even if you won't do it for me, I hope you'll do it for him."

Eva stuck a finger down her throat and made a gagging sound, but she stood up slowly.

"Fine. I'll go as far as meeting him. But no promises after that."

Shiloh nodded and trudged back up the hill without looking to see if Eva was following.

CHAPTER 12

A blanket of choking damp warmth engulfed Shiloh as she stepped from the vent into the woods of Rock Creek Park.

"Yuck. It's only June, isn't it? Why does it have to be so hot?"

Shiloh shrugged. She knew better than to mention global warming. Another topic her teenage daughter was sick of hearing about. As they walked toward Josh's townhouse Shiloh wondered if it would ever get any better between her and Eva. Even on the brief trip back to Earth the conflict between mother and daughter chafed like a new blister. Shiloh had a feeling it wouldn't take much to make it burst.

As they came in sight of the house, Shiloh stole a peek at Eva's face, hoping to see some softening of her hostility. Eva's jaw was set and there was an angry light in her eye. She lagged behind as Shiloh went to the door.

Shiloh tried the knob. It was locked. She knocked, and after a long minute Josh opened the door. The look on his face was guarded, though Shiloh detected relief in his eyes when he glanced over her shoulder at Eva.

"What do you want?" he said.

"Can we come in?" Shiloh asked.

He stared at her for a few seconds before stepping away to let them pass. The living room was dark and quiet, the air stale and warm.

Josh stood and watched them, waiting.

Eva glanced from Shiloh to Josh. She shook her head impatiently and said, "If you two won't talk, I will. We're looking for my dad. Has he been here?"

"He was here," Josh said.

Watching him, Shiloh felt a dull knife twist in her gut. "I'm sorry to bring all of this back to you," she said.

Josh snorted. "You think it ever went away? Do you think I don't worry about both of you every day?" He turned away and collected himself. "He came a week after you left. If I'd had a way to contact you, I would have."

"Where is he now?" Eva asked.

"I'm not sure. He might be in North Carolina." He turned to Shiloh. "Your father sent a message. He said Forest was staying at the house, hoping you'd show up there."

"When was that?" she asked.

"Last week."

"Let's go," Eva said, heading for the door.

"Wait," Shiloh called after her.

Eva stopped at the door and glared back at Shiloh, who was staring at Josh. He had the crumpled, wasted look of someone who hadn't slept in a while. "Are you okay?" Shiloh asked.

"Forget me. That should be easy for you. You've had enough practice."

"I said I'm sorry."

"Yeah. You're good at that."

"Wah, wah," Eva mocked. "You're both pathetic. Life is hard. Get over it." She glowered at Shiloh. "We made a deal. You take me to meet my dad, and then we're done. You can come back here and patch things up with Mr. Lonely after I'm gone. Let's go."

Shiloh would have argued with her, but this wasn't the time to talk with Josh anyway. Instead she asked, "Is there a car I could borrow?"

"A car?" Eva wailed. "Why can't we just vent there?"

Shiloh gave her a thin smile and said, "I miss driving. Road trips."

"I don't get it," Eva said.

"That's because you've never been on one," Shiloh said.

Josh went into another room and came back with a key. "It's a solar. Not the fastest, but it runs."

"I'll bring it back," she said.

"Do what you have to do," he said.

He led them outside into the damp summer evening and showed them the small car. It was about as stylish as a refrigerator.

Eva gaped at it. "Good grief. You're kidding, right?" she said.

Shiloh hugged Josh and thanked him. Then she looked at Eva and said, "Get in, sit down, shut up, and hold on."

***

The weeds weren't too bad until they got past Richmond. The old pavement on I-95 had held up pretty well. But as they got closer to the North Carolina border, the dock and chicory stalks were wiry as chain link fence. Once or twice the roughage was so thick it clogged in the wheel wells, forcing Shiloh to get out and hack at it with the tire iron while Eva stood fuming by the side of the road.

"Why can't you just magic it away?" she complained.

"I don't know a spell for weed control. Believe me, I wish I did," Shiloh grumbled, wiping her sweaty hands on her pants.

Eva smirked at her. "Are you ready to find a vent?"

Shiloh turned back to the tire. "I've almost got it loose."

"Until the next time." Eva shook her head. "I still don't see why you think this is such a great experience. We could be there now."

Shiloh grunted with satisfaction and stood up, waving the gnats away from her face. "Aw, but then we wouldn't have these magical moments together."

Eva grimaced. "You call this magic?"

"It ain't all abracadabra, kid," Shiloh said, getting back in the car.

Later, after Eva fell asleep as they crawled along a former four-lane highway reduced to one by invading weeds, Shiloh stole a glance at the stranger her daughter had become. In the three days they'd been together they hadn't had a single meaningful conversation. Eva responded to every remark with sarcasm or contempt. Shiloh tried to remember if she had ever been as hostile to her own parents. But there was no point in thinking about it, she told herself. The world had changed. She had changed. How could she have imagined her daughter wouldn't change?

And the nearer they got to her parents' home, the less hopeful she felt that anything positive would come from Eva meeting Forest. If he were there.

A sudden flash of the last time she'd seen him broke Shiloh's concentration. She felt a chill recalling the confusion and pain in his face when he realized she was leaving.

And yet, they'd never had a real relationship. Their time together in Theatros had been so short and unreal. They never got past the honeymoon stage before it went straight to hell. Do not pass Go, do not collect two hundred dollars.

She sighed. Eva's two-tone hair had fallen across her face. Her cheekbones were all Forest. Shiloh wondered what else was swimming in her daughter's gene pool. If some part of Jack was in her...

Eva opened one eye and caught Shiloh looking at her. "Keep your eyes on the road, Mom," she said.

Shiloh gripped the wheel tighter and swerved to avoid a snake slithering across the cracked pavement.

It was almost sundown when they finally pulled into the clearing in front of her parents' house. Since her mother's death three years earlier, her father had expanded the vegetable garden. Shiloh opened the car door carefully to avoid hitting a squash patch.

When she looked up, Forest was standing on the porch staring at her. He was gaunt and pale, his beard threaded with silver, but the dark light in his eyes still fell on her with an intensity that made her stumble.

"You must be him." Eva said. She stood on the other side of the car, watching Forest looking at her mother.

Forest continued staring at Shiloh until she frowned and said, "Forest, I'd like you to meet our daughter."

He turned his head slowly, as if unwilling to take his eyes off Shiloh. "Hello," he said.

"Hi," Eva said, a world of indifference in her tone.

Shiloh rolled her eyes. "So. Here we are. One small happy family."

"Cut it out, Mom."

"Fine. Whatever. I'm going to find Grandpa."

"Your father is making a meal inside. We didn't know when... if... you would get here." Forest's voice slipped under Shiloh's skin. She felt a dizzying rush, as if the sands of time were being sucked back into the sea, and she was in danger of losing her footing. She scrambled for purchase and fled up the porch steps and into the house.

Brendan Carter was at the stove, stirring something fragrant with browned onions and herbs. He turned at the sound of her footsteps and closed the distance between them.

Released from his hug, Shiloh looked into his dark brown eyes and said softly, "You okay, Dad?"

He nodded. "Good days, bad days. I get along all right."

Shiloh tried to stop herself from looking around to see her mother. This room would always be the one place her spirit remained strongest.

"He seems a fine young man," Brendan said.

"Oh. Not so young anymore." Shiloh said.

"Everyone looks young when you get to my age," he replied.

"Eva's here, too."

"Ah. She, at least, is truly young."

Shiloh frowned.

"What?" Brendan asked.

Shiloh sighed heavily. "Oh, you know. Kids grow up too fast. And she's..."

"If she's still like you, you'll be all right. She'll come through it."

"I hope you're right."

"Oh, gag me." Eva stood in the doorway with the air of someone about to catch a plane.

"Hi Grandpa," she said. When he smiled at her something shifted in the room, as if years of uncertainty fell away, and something bright and sure as childhood's first love flared for a moment.

"It smells good. I guess Grandma taught you how to cook, huh?"

They sat down to a simple meal of eggs and potatoes with fresh salad, some berries and cream for dessert. Amidst the clatter of forks and spoons and the gleam of candlelight Eva let down her guard slightly. She watched Forest watching Shiloh, who was focused on her own father. No one asked Eva any questions.

As the last berry disappeared from the bowl, Brendan Carter leaned back in his chair and asked Shiloh, "So, what's next for you? More dragons to slay? Or genies to bottle up?"

Shiloh shrugged. "It's a job."

Brendan shook his head with a smile. "I don't know how you manage. Even around here we see a lot more strangeness than ever before. I don't mean to criticize, but I have to wonder."

"What do you mean?" Shiloh asked.

"You said your job was to keep the magic from getting into the wrong hands. I'm afraid that battle's lost."

Shiloh nodded. "I know. I can't keep ahead of it anymore. Honestly, I think they knew it was only a matter of time before the magic got loose. The hope is that if we can sort of police it—you know—maybe we can limit the craziness."

"Earth is doomed." Forest intoned this with such glum gravity that Shiloh couldn't help laughing.

"See, this is why you shouldn't be here," she said. "Only people crazy enough to believe in the impossible belong on Earth."

Brendan looked at Forest sympathetically and said, "Just because we're all going to die doesn't mean Earth is doomed."

"I'm not talking about death," Forest said. "I'm talking about balance. The harmony of nature. The natural order that keeps rain falling and grass growing. The instincts and intuition that have guided all the creatures on the planet for millennia are being wiped out in a matter of a few decades."

"That may be so," Brendan said. "But some will survive. Some will carry on. Life will go on."

"But will it be worth living?" Forest asked.

"You guys make me sick. Just because things have changed since you were young doesn't mean they've gotten worse. There's magic now. That's a good thing. There's nothing we can't do. We can fix everything that's wrong and punish everyone who's evil." Eva's eyes burned bright with conviction as she challenged the adults.

Shiloh shook her head gently. "But honey, what about when evil people learn how to do magic?"

"I'll fix 'em."

Brendan smiled at this, but Forest and Shiloh exchanged the worried glance of parents. Eva caught them at it and flared up.

"You don't think I can. I know. You think I'm just a kid and I don't know anything."

"No, that's not true. I know you're special. And I know you've learned something about magic. But it's not as easy as it seems. And lately..." Shiloh paused, then continued, "It's getting so much harder. I thought when I started this, back before you were born—I thought it would get easier. Maybe just fade away. But it's getting stronger—the magic—almost like it's getting smarter. I don't know how much more I can do."

"You need help," Brendan said. "You should ask them— the ones who gave you the job. They should send you reinforcements."

"Maybe I will."

"Magda won't help you," Eva said. "She doesn't care about you anymore. But she loves me. I could ask her."

Shiloh gaped at her daughter.

"But I won't," Eva continued smugly. "If you're tired of doing your job you should quit. That's what people do. It won't matter soon anyway. I'm going to be in charge, and I'll take care of everything. You'll see."

The three adults stared at the cocky teenager, but not one of them spoke.

After Eva left the room, Brendan said goodnight. Shiloh and Forest were left alone together in a silence sticky as tar. She tried not to show how irritated she felt at the way he was staring at her. But she didn't have the energy to waste.

"You never should have come here."

He flinched slightly. "You should have told me about her."

"Let's not go through all of that. You've seen her now. Do you really think she would have turned out differently if you'd been here the whole time?"

"I don't know." He stared into the fire. "She doesn't like me."

Shiloh shook her head. "She doesn't like anyone. She's a teenager. And she's just found out she can do magic, so..." Shiloh sighed. "She's like the teenager from hell."

"She reminds me of you."

"Gee, thanks."

"You know what I mean. She's beautiful, and she has that...fire." He stared intently at her.

Shiloh sighed again and said, "Listen. You and me? That's over. You and Eva? I don't know, but if I had to guess, I'd say she's not going to go out on a limb for you. If you want to connect with her, you're going to have to meet her more than halfway."

"She's not interested in me anymore. The magic in her veins is like a drug. You and I mean nothing to her. But...I hoped you might feel..."

"I'm sorry. It's been thirteen years. A lot's happened. I don't have time for that kind of stuff anymore. It's just not important." She shrugged. "I'm not sorry about us, or Eva, even though she's a pain now. I just hope she doesn't get herself killed before she grows up."

Forest nodded. "Do you want me go?"

"Don't go without talking to her first. I mean, she came here to meet you. I think you should give her a chance to ask any questions she has. And, you know, show her that you care."

"I'm here."

"That's not enough. She doesn't know you. She might think you came to see me."

His haunted stare turned darker. Shiloh felt chills on the back of her neck, but she betrayed nothing in her face.

"Lyra loves you," she said.

"I've tried to be good to her."

"Well...keep trying."

He stood up. "I'll say goodbye to Eva in the morning," he said, and turned to the hall.

"Forest?"

He stopped and looked back at her.

"Thanks for coming. Thanks for..." she began and halted.

His face was unreadable in the darkness. He left without another word.

***

When Shiloh came downstairs in the morning her father was alone at the kitchen table.

"Eva's still asleep?" she asked.

Brendan tilted his head toward the window, and Shiloh saw the girl slouching in the yard, listening to Forest. It looked like he was doing most of the talking. Shiloh felt a pang of sympathy for him. But even as she watched him trying to win Eva over, Shiloh felt how unimportant it was for him to do so. The breaking of the parent-child bond, or at least the loosening of it, was inevitable. Maybe it was too bad that she had denied Forest the chance to know his daughter, but it was damage done. Regret wouldn't help any of them.

Yet she kept watching, waiting for some sign of softening in Eva's stance. None came. Shiloh sighed.

"You shouldn't worry about either of them. They'll be fine. He has other children who need him more than she does." Brendan spoke quietly, but his words still carried weight in Shiloh's heart. She shot a smile at him.

"You seem to be doing okay on your own, Dad."

He shrugged. "I get along. So many people are worse off. And your mother told me not to fall apart after she was gone." He studied Shiloh for a moment. "She was proud of you."

"Thanks, Dad. I don't think I've done such a great job. But I'm not giving up."

"That's all we can do." He glanced back out the window. Forest was attempting to hug Eva. She appeared to be tolerating it. Then he stepped back and headed toward the woods behind the house.

"Where will you and Eva go when you leave here?" Brendan asked.

Shiloh poured herself a cup of coffee and sat down at the table. "How'd you get this coffee?"

"There's a couple of guys down the street who run a route to Guatemala on horseback. They make good money."

"I'm surprised they haven't been robbed."

"They were, a few times. No one is safe."

Shiloh stared out the window, watching Eva lingering by the dogs. After a minute she said, "I don't know what she's gonna do. I can't stay at home with her. And she's already made it clear she's not going to stay with Josh. I'm afraid she's going to go back to Magda and try to become some kind of badass witch."

Brendan nodded. "Yes. She seems taken with the idea of power. It's understandable. But...I wonder..."

"What?"

"Well, it may be natural for a girl her age to resist the influence of her parents. Even to resist the influence of friends—though from what I've seen it's not clear that she has any friends. But if she doesn't care about anyone..."

"I know. I've been thinking about that too. I'm worried that she doesn't seem to care about anyone or anything except magic."

"What would you think if I gave her a puppy?"

"I'd worry about the puppy."

Brendan nodded. "It may not work. But if she doesn't learn to care for something outside herself, she could be lost to us. And to herself, really."

"Well, when you put it like that... Do you have a puppy handy?"

"A woman down the street has a litter of mutts. They're old enough to leave their mother." He gave Shiloh a look. "They start biting her when they're ready."

Chapter 13

Shiloh crumpled the note in her hand and jammed it into her back pocket before she walked up to Josh's door. Her first instinct had been to use it as an opener, perhaps gain his sympathy. At least soften him up before she tried to heal the breach between them.

But as she parked the car she realized he wouldn't be surprised that Eva had run away again. He probably saw it coming long before she did. It had been gnawing at Shiloh on the slow return trip. She couldn't kid herself anymore. Seeing Forest in the flesh had been a revelation. She had thought she would feel something, after all they'd been through. But even though he was as handsome as ever—in some ways more so; sorrow became him—Shiloh found herself comparing him to Josh. It was the thought of Josh—sweet, smart, patient, and altogether mortal—that sustained her and gave her the strength to send Forest away for good.

She braced herself and knocked on the door. It opened slowly. He stood blinking at her like a man roused suddenly from a deep sleep.

"I brought your car back," she said after a few seconds.

He was barefoot, wearing a wrinkled button-down shirt and jeans that looked as if he'd slept in them. He stared at her blankly. She couldn't tell if he was angry or just indifferent.

"I can go if you're busy... If this is a bad time—"

He reached out and grabbed her wrist. "Don't go."

She saw it then, in his eyes.

She took a step closer, leaning in to hug him. He put his arms around her and buried his face in her hair. She held onto him and let go of everything else.

Later, after they'd said the things that needed to be said, and she'd told him how Eva had run away again, they made some food and ate together and talked until they fell asleep. And the next morning they began anew.

Josh showed her his latest reports on the spreading magic threats.

"Is it just me, or is this getting worse faster than before?" she asked, scrolling down a list of incidents from all corners of the Earth.

Josh shook his head. "It's almost completely out of control. The military can't cope with it. No jets, limited munitions. But it's almost worse in the places with independent militias. Those guys are nuts. They try to bring down dragons with rocket launchers and all they do is make the dragons angry."

"That would explain these accounts of whole counties burning?"

"Yeah. Some of the dragons seem to be working together. If one of them gets hurt, ten more show up and retaliate. And they don't run out of fire."

"Oh, hell." Shiloh slumped in her chair and threw up her hands. "That's it then, isn't it? I mean. It's turning into chaos. I can't stop that."

Josh sighed and shrugged. "I don't know. Lately I've been thinking maybe the dragons are on our side. So far they haven't attacked any towns or villages. If they wanted to scare people or wipe them out, they could do it. But they're not. So, I'm thinking maybe..." He shrugged again.

"Have you said this to Colby? Or anyone else?"

"No. They're all totally freaked out by the dragons. They understand guns and grenades. They still think we're in a war against magic. But we've lost that—if we ever were in a war. I'm not so sure anymore."

"Does this mean I don't have to go back out there and try to put out the fires?"

"If you're asking me, I'd like to get a sailboat and live on it until all of this settles down."

Shiloh grinned. "Really? You think we'd be safe on a sailboat?"

"Sure. We could go up to the Pacific Northwest and sail around the islands in Puget Sound. There's plenty of fish. No hurricanes to worry about. From what I've seen in the wires, the worst fighting is in the Midwest and the Deep South."

"What would we do for money?"

"Same as everybody else these days. Barter stuff. Live by our wits."

Later they watched the daily news broadcast on a small television that picked up the last functioning satellite channel in the District. Since advertising revenue had all but vanished after the meltdown of international travel and marketing, the technical polish of earlier video feeds had declined considerably, but the station was still able to broadcast news stories in a primitive fashion.

The show began with a report on a breakout of vandalism in a remote Virginia county where gangs of so-called "hoppers"—young men under the influence of an alcoholic beverage produced from hops grown in magic-contaminated soil—had gone on a rampage, burning, looting and "rebooting"—using magic to inflict tails and horns on innocent bystanders. The "reboots" were expected to revert back to normal, the broadcaster said, but Shiloh shook her head in doubt. She glanced at Josh.

"I know what you're thinking," he said.

"What?"

"You think you have to stop them."

"Well? Don't you think they need to be stopped?"

"Sure. But for every one of those punks that you stop, a dozen more are going to be doing things just as bad or worse. You can't fix them all."

"How I can I walk away? Who else can do it?"

Josh was staring at the television, where the image had turned to a story about a woman raising winged horses who was planning to launch a local air-service business.

"Couldn't you train some other people to work with you?"

"I don't really know how to do that without injecting them with some Deep Magic first. And that's too risky. Look at Eva. She was a good kid, but now she's got all this power and..." Shiloh stared off into space with the expression of someone watching a huge fiery comet approaching.

The knot tightened in her gut as she tried to steel herself against her greatest fear: the day she would be called upon to put down some upstart enchantress who turned out to be her daughter.

PART TWO

CHAPTER 14

After leaving her mother behind a second time, Eva spent two years with Magda, absorbing all the knowledge the queen offered. The girl learned so quickly and displayed such an appetite for power that Magda soon came to the uncomfortable realization that Eva had the potential to take over before the queen was ready to relinquish her throne.

By the time she was fifteen Eva was aware that Magda was trying to slow her down. The girl pretended she didn't notice while the queen continued the charade of mentoring. When, just before her sixteenth birthday, Eva announced that she was leaving, Magda made no attempt to discourage her.

And after the girl had left the castle, the old queen changed the magical locks.

Eva took a dragon through the vents on her return to Earth. She still had the dog her grandfather had given her. Mudley had his own special harness to keep him from falling off the dragon's broad back, and he yapped excitedly as they rode. When they emerged into the steamy midsummer jungle of what used to be Ohio, Mudley snapped at the fist-sized mosquitoes and crunchy June bugs.

"Don't make yourself sick eating those," Eva warned, looking back at the mutt. "You'll have better things to chase soon."

Mudley wagged his tail and barked.

Eva had never tried to teach him any tricks. It was nice to have one friend whose simplicity wasn't feigned.

In Magda's castle Eva had learned to avoid friendships. Elves were completely untrustworthy in any case, and the humans she'd met since she came into her power all acted weird around her—either too afraid to be truthful or too stupid to realize she could tell they were lying. She had no patience for it. Mudley was her best friend.

Now, staring out at the cliffs above the Hudson River and envisioning a castle, she felt the irksome drag of gravity. She couldn't wave a castle into existence. She'd tried to get Magda to give her the skills, but the older woman had been coy on that front. After much nagging, Magda had finally relented enough to give Eva a wand. Without adequate instruction about how to use it, she'd found the wand an unreliable tool at best. She was sure if she had the manual she'd be flying solo and conjuring glass castles out of thin air by now, but so far, the wand had proven to be more of a fashion statement than a power tool. Yet Eva couldn't stomach the idea of crawling back to Magda to ask for help.

She would find her own way of doing things. She woke each day with a growing sensation of magical power tingling in her veins. She simply needed practice.

She picked up a rock and threw it out into the river, recalling the moment of her first transformative act. If only she knew how to to kick it up a few hundred notches.

Oh well, she thought. If she couldn't do it the easy way, she would just have to make it happen the human way. Luckily, she had no trouble conjuring money; it worked almost like magic on humans anyway.

***

Clayton rolled over on the ground and pulled the blanket tighter, but his shivering continued. He opened his eyes wearily and looked at the tree where he had tied the horse the night before.

He blinked and sat up with a lurch. He swiveled his head, hoping if the horse had slipped loose it would still be lingering nearby. A quick glance around the campsite confirmed what he already guessed.

The man who had sold him the horse back in Missouri had warned him that thieves were ruthless on the highways. For months Clayton had been careful to find campsites away from the roads. He must have made a mistake last night.

He was grateful they hadn't taken his guitar. He could keep going on foot. He would have been lost without the guitar.

It had taken him more than a year to make the decision to leave the only home he'd ever known. After Eva left, Clayton had tried to forget her, since it was clear she wasn't interested in him anyway. He tried to lose himself in playing the guitar. The plan worked, but not quite the way he'd expected. In the music that sprang to life at his touch he discovered consolation inside himself. He didn't know if he was any good. He only knew that when he played the guitar his life made some kind of sense. The music eased the pain he had grown accustomed to wearing like a lead vest. He began to think he might have some sort of future.

Thus, two years after Eva vanished from his sight, Clayton had sold what he could of his possessions and left the house in the care of a young couple who promised to watch over his parents' graves. He bought a horse, and headed East. Eva had mentioned that her mother lived in D.C.. Clayton had no idea how long it would take him to get there, or if he would be able to find Eva, but at least he had a plan. Sketchy, perhaps, but something with a pointy end to follow.

As the realization that the horse was really gone sank in, he gathered his bedroll and his pack, strapped his guitar on his back, and resumed his trek on foot.

A couple of hours later he stopped at a crossroads where a few weathered buildings huddled under large bare trees. One of the buildings had a handmade sign in the window that read, "No Loitering."

Clayton snorted in amusement. The place looked completely deserted. He wondered what had led the owners to post such a seemingly unnecessary sign.

He went inside and found that it was a grocery with more bare shelves than food. He bought a biscuit, and asked the woman who sold it to him if they had much trouble with loiterers.

The woman pursed her lips and looked Clayton up and down before she answered. "You got a guitar," she said flatly.

"Yes, I do," he admitted.

She considered this for a moment. "You don't look like a gypsy."

Clayton arched one eyebrow. "No, ma'am. I'm not a gypsy, I don't think. I don't know what they look like."

"They jingle. They stand around and smile over nothing and steal whatever they can. They loiter." The woman looked over Clayton's shoulder as she said this.

He turned and saw a man in the doorway wearing a battered fedora and a bandana knotted around his neck. A wide white mustache drooped to frame his mouth. The man nodded slightly to the woman.

The woman glared at the him and said, "Go on. We don't want your kind around here."

"Ah, I'm sorry if I or my people have given offense. None was intended, I assure you. I want only to buy a bag of flour so my wife can feed our children." The man had a melodious voice, and Clayton couldn't help smiling at his old-fashioned way of speaking, though he wondered if it was all an act.

"Show me your money," the woman demanded.

The man pulled out some coins and laid them on the counter. The woman inspected them carefully. "Is that all you got?" she asked.

"Sadly, yes," the man said.

"I can give you four pounds of flour for this. No more," she said.

The man accepted the flour and left the store, nodding at Clayton as he passed him.

Clayton hurried after him. On the road outside two horse-drawn wooden covered wagons waited. They were painted colorfully with arcane symbols and flowery motifs. A woman sat on the seat holding the reins of one. A man and a girl who looked to be in her teens occupied the driver's seat of the other. Clayton stared at the horses. He didn't think either of them was his. Still...

He went up to the man who had come into the store and said, "Excuse me. Do you have any room in your wagon for another passenger? I lost my horse last night and I could really use a ride."

The man looked at him with raised eyebrows. "You lost your horse?"

Clayton shrugged. "I'm trying to get back East. Are you headed that way?"

The man eyed the guitar strapped to Clayton's back. "You are a musician?"

"Yes," Clayton said, with an air of confidence he hoped was convincing.

The man smiled. "We also are musicians. Perhaps we can play together. You may ride with us to our next camp. There we will play and see if we make beautiful music together."

"Okay," Clayton said, climbing up and into the wagon, where three small children watched him with wide eyes. The wagon started moving with a rolling shake and clatter, and Clayton wondered if he would regret this decision. One of the little girls smiled at him. He smiled back. So far, so good.

The novelty of riding in the wagon wore off quickly, and when the children dozed Clayton found it difficult to keep his eyes open. But he was wary of sleeping in this company of strangers, so he forced himself to stay alert and passed the hours staring out the small windows in the sides of the wagon.

As the sun drew near the horizon, the wagon turned off the road. Clayton saw that they had entered a small field where several other wagons were gathered in a loose circle. When they came to a stop he climbed down the small set of steps at the back and gazed around.

There was a campfire well underway. Some women were cooking; others were talking in small groups. The man with the mustache came up to Clayton and said, "My name is Theo. What shall we call you?"

"My name is Clayton."

"You can choose a new name if you want. We won't care. We are a free people." He looked around the campsite and noticed Clayton eyeing the campfire. "You must be hungry. We will eat first. Then you can tell us who you are, and who you want to be."

Clayton was relieved to be offered food before he had to answer such questions. At this point he had more questions than answers.

The bowl of savory meat stew he was given tasted like nothing he'd ever eaten, but it was the best food he'd had since he started out on the road. He glanced at the woman who had served it to him and smiled at her. She eyed him thoughtfully for a moment, then turned to Theo with a questioning gaze.

Theo ignored this until he had finished his meal. Then he looked around the group gathered in the firelight and said, "This is Clayton. He is a musician of some sort. He is our guest this night. Tomorrow, who knows?"

One of the younger men sitting across the circle said, "Where are you from? Where are you going?"

Clayton answered, "I'm from Missouri. I'm heading east. Looking for...I don't know. Work, I guess."

"What kind of work?"

Clayton didn't see who asked this, but he answered anyway. "I don't know. I'd like to work as a musician, but I don't know if I'm good enough."

Theo nodded. "You must be good to earn a living at music. Play something for us. We can tell you if you have a chance, because our people have always been musicians."

"What sort of song would you like to hear?" Clayton asked, feeling somewhat shy at being the sudden focus of attention.

"Play your favorite song," Theo suggested.

Clayton got out his guitar and thought for a moment. He didn't think he had a favorite song, but he did have one he always played first, to warm up his fingers, so he started with it.

"Pack up all my cares and woes, here I come, singing low, Bye, bye, blackbird..."

As soon as he began, the three children who had ridden in the wagon with him scuttled closer and watched him intently. He played it twice through because it was so short, and he wanted to give them time to make up their minds about him. When he finished the last chord he looked up. The gypsies were watching him, as if waiting for something else to happen.

Theo nodded solemnly. "This is your favorite song?"

"Oh, well, it's a song I like. I don't really have a favorite. I don't think."

Theo clapped his hands together and barked a loud laugh, at the sound of which all the rest of the gypsies smiled and nodded.

"You see?" Theo said to Clayton, gesturing to the faces lit by firelight. "They were puzzled by this song of yours, as was I. This sort of song... It is all right. It is not terrible. But it would never be anyone's favorite song. A favorite song can only be one of two things: very sad or very happy. Because only songs which are very sad, or very happy, speak to our hearts. If you want to be a musician—a real musician—you must make people feel something. It can be sad or happy, makes no difference. Sometimes sad is a good feeling. Sometimes happiness makes you cry. But only music that makes you feel these things is true music. If it doesn't, it is just songs, like children sing."

Theo looked around the campfire at the others, some of whom were nodding in agreement. Then he lifted his chin toward a bearded man sitting between two pretty women across the circle. "Ramone, show our guest how to play a sad song."

Someone handed Ramone a guitar, and the circle hushed expectantly.

Clayton focused on the man's fingers, hoping to learn some technique. But when Ramone began his fingers moved with such delicacy and speed, his touch so sure and light, that Clayton was dazzled before the man even began singing. The song was one Clayton had never heard, which didn't surprise him, but he felt as if he must have heard it before, because it rang so true and pure. It was about the love of a young girl for a thoughtless youth, who took her for granted and never realized that she was the love of his life until it was too late and she had died with a broken heart. The haunting melody expressed the pain of regret and the anguish of loss so eloquently that tears rose to Clayton's eyes. As he hastily wiped them away he noticed that others in the circle also wept.

When the song ended, Clayton inclined his head to Ramone and said "Thank you. That was beautiful."

"Yes," said Theo. "That was sorrow. Now, give us joy."

Ramone bent to the task and in less time than Clayton would have believed possible, the mood in the circle lifted to one of celebration. The song rose on a circle of notes that seemed to continually spiral upward. Clayton didn't understand the lyrics, but he saw that many of the gypsies were singing along on the chorus with smiling faces, and when the song came to a rousing finish a spontaneous cheer erupted.

"And that," said Theo, "is how to win an audience."

Clayton shook his head, grinning. "I don't know if I could ever learn to play like that. But I'll try."

Later, after he told the gypsies that he was aiming for Washington, D.C., they welcomed him to travel with them as far as Philadelphia. But after that they would be turning north.

"We don't go near the government. They don't like our people," Theo explained.

That night Clayton slept under the stars, but he felt more secure than he had in months. He realized there was a chance that he might be robbed in his sleep. But when he thought of the music Ramone had played, and the way the people had responded to it, he couldn't believe such people would take advantage of him. Anyway, he didn't have much left. And they already had better guitars than his.

In the weeks that followed Clayton learned a lot about the way the gypsies carried themselves through the broken world. They never lacked for food, though they owned little. They were skillful at recognizing opportunities and winning over audiences. Whenever they came near a small town they would send in one wagon first, to test the mood of the locals. If they seemed friendly, they would ask for permission to camp at the edge of town. And once they'd set up their camp, the locals, no matter how skeptical or dismissive at the start, sooner or later gave in to curiosity. The lure of music, the scent of unfamiliar cooking, and the bold glances of the dark-eyed beauties who ventured into the towns to trade tempted even the most reserved citizens.

Clayton tried to make himself useful to the group, although at first he felt embarrassed when he tried to fit in. The young gypsy girls seemed to find amusement in his every word and act. They teased him constantly.

"The only way to make them stop is to pick one and make her your girl," said Gregor, one of the older boys. Gregor played the accordion, and had an easy way with women of all ages. The older ones enjoyed his flattery while the younger ones fought for his attention. He was sitting next to Clayton at the evening campfire when he offered his advice.

"I don't want a girlfriend," Clayton said. "I'm not going to live this life forever."

"No one lives forever," Gregor said. "You pick a girl for now. For tonight. Tomorrow maybe you pick another."

"I don't want to do that," Clayton said. "It's not fair to them. Besides," he added, "I'm not really a gypsy."

Gregor sniffed. "Who is? Half the people here are no more gypsy than you. Only Ramone and Theo and Griselle are true Romany. The rest of us joined up just like you. Because we wanted the lifestyle. Freedom. Travel. Adventure." He studied Clayton's face. "You telling me you don't want all of that?"

Clayton stared into the fire for a minute. "I do and I don't." He paused, and then said, "There was this girl..."

"Hah!" Gregor laughed. "There's always a girl. And another girl. That's my point."

"But this girl—"

"She was special," Gregor interrupted. He shook his head. Then he smiled and said, "That's cool. So you're looking for Special Girl?"

"I guess so. I didn't think I was when I left, but... Yeah. I'm looking for her."

"And you think she's waiting for you?"

Clayton shrugged. "I don't know if she even remembers me."

Gregor nodded. "So, hopeless romance. That's a gypsy thing. Maybe you're more gypsy than you know."

CHAPTER 15

Jack was bored. Ever since he'd sent Jessie to Rufio he'd missed the stimulating friction of conflict. No one had the nerve to argue with him anymore. And Earth, once his playground, had fallen into such a chaotic state that it was no place for a vacation. The last time he had visited New Orleans, even the Mardi Gras atmosphere of that great city had lost its playful appeal. After a brief fling with a winsome waitress, Jack had no desire to linger.

Still, he enjoyed keeping an eye on Shiloh and her little friend Josh. It amused Jack to watch Shiloh attempting to stop the rampant spread of Deep Magic. Had Jack been human he might have felt a twinge of guilt about the mayhem he'd brought upon Earth. But happily for him, he was devoid of conscience.

Opening the vision portal he had locked on Shiloh's mortal signature, he clapped his hands with glee to discover her locked in combat with a band of trollish goons. They didn't look like any trolls he'd ever seen before, but then, since the Greening all sorts of hybrid freaks were kicking up trouble. Shiloh continued to amaze Jack with her resourcefulness and courage. Few men would have welcomed a fight against super-sized opponents displaying such brainless ferocity, yet Shiloh had them on their heels. She was brandishing a whip of some sort with a sizzling edge that reduced the trolls to bite-size pieces. It was all over in a few minutes. Jack sighed contentedly and turned away, starting at the discovery that he was not alone.

"This is how you spend your time?"

Jack bridled at the disdain in Cyrene's voice.

"Why shouldn't I?" he responded, standing up in an effort to face the sea queen eye-to-eye.

Cyrene snorted derisively. "Oh Jack. Sometimes I wonder how you stay in charge over here. You're so lazy."

Jack smiled. Cyrene never worried him the way Magda did. The sea queen's temper was ever more placid. She might be condescending at times, but Jack knew Cyrene would never try to take his head off. Unlike some.

"You're looking lovely as always, Cyrene. May I ask what brings you here? It's been a while."

"Yes. Well. I've been busy with affairs of sea. Perhaps you haven't noticed the change in the currents?"

Jack shrugged. "Isn't that normal? Tides, currents, all that sort of thing? Is there a problem?"

Cyrene flared her nostrils and lowered her chin. "Yes, Jack. There's a problem."

He shrugged again. "How does this affect me?"

Cyrene let out an exasperated sigh. "Of course. It's not a problem unless it affects you."

"No need for sarcasm, dear. I'm simply telling you, if there's a problem, it's news to me. Is it something to do with Vesuvius? I heard he was venting again. Such a blowhard. I don't know how you put up with him."

Cyrene tapped her foot impatiently. "We don't have time for gossip, Jack. There are graver issues to consider. The rogue girl, for one."

"If you're referring to Shiloh, she's hardly a rogue. She works for us, as I recall."

"Don't pretend you know nothing about the offspring. We're all aware of your penchant for playing innocent, but there's nothing innocent about this unholy child."

"Really? What a delightful turn of events."

"You laugh now, but I fear the little witch is brewing trouble beyond her ken. There's a rumor in the currents that Gaia is stirring. You—up here with your head in the trees— can't feel it. But beneath the waves, the sensation is unmistakable. The seas are rising, the cracks in the ocean floor are widening."

"So? All that has happened before."

"Not like this. This time we can feel the stinging bite of panic in the very water we breathe. The Mother is weeping briny tears of rage. I don't think we can soothe her with mere human sacrifice this time. She may feel the need to erase Theatros in the bargain."

"Oh, come now. She always loved us best."

"We were supposed to take care of the other Earth. And we have failed."

"In what way? I got rid of their foul pollution and reduced the overpopulation considerably. I stopped them messing about with nuclear forces. What more does She want?"

"The Mother only knows. All I can tell you is, She's not happy now."

"If that's why you're here, shouldn't Magda and Rufio be included in the discussion?"

"They're as bad as the earthlings. Magda loves fighting almost as much as Rufio. Gaia has been patient with their nonsense for centuries, but the latest news from Earth suggests that the containment strategy isn't working. We could be witnessing another episode of chemagical mayhem if we don't intervene swiftly and effectively. And when I say we, I mean you and I. Much as we may not agree on other issues, you at least understand the vital role of harmony and balance in life on Theatros and Earth. So I'm asking you to set aside your selfish amusement and consider how amusing life will be when all of this is underwater."

"You think She'd do that?"

"She's done it before."

"Yes, but that was so long ago, before we were even properly split into two worlds. She wouldn't flush us away the way She did Earth."

"Is that really a gamble you want to take?"

Jack turned to the window and stared out. "I suppose not." He snapped off a tendril of vine curling over the window ledge and started idly weaving it into a crown. "What do you propose?"

Cyrene took hold of his hand and led him to the basin nearby. She waved her vision scepter over the water. As an image floated to the surface she said, "Here's where I think we should start."

***

Eva gazed at the sunlight sparkling on the river where her fleet of pirate ships bobbed and fluttered like bridesmaids fitted out for the big day. They were beautiful and restless, waiting for their chance to show what they could do.

Eva allowed herself a moment of quiet pride. Magda had warned her that she needed more lessons, more practice. She hadn't said more maturity, but Eva had heard the unspoken critique. The queen's silent disapproval only made her more determined to prove that she could establish her own realm on Earth. As it turned out, it had been ridiculously easy.

Humanity was in such disarray, struggling to maintain some semblance of civilized order, that Eva was able to take charge with hardly a whisper of resistance. It helped that she'd chosen her spot well. In this particular region, the infrastructure had been crumbling long before The Greening finished it off. The few people still clinging to their homes overlooking the Hudson River were weakened by hunger and the harsh weather, which swung wildly between smothering heat in the summer and paralyzing storms in the winter.

Snug in her castle by the time the first storm hit, Eva hadn't minded the snow at all. In truth, she had come this far north in defiance of one of Magda's oft repeated maxims.

"Don't ever think you can control the weather," she would say, whenever Eva made some careless remark about the future. "Weather is the plaything of the gods. They have no mercy for ambitious fools."

Eva had kept her thoughts to herself, but she vowed that she would never allow a weather report to stop her. When she was ready, she would conquer as much of the planet as she wanted. Rain or shine.

True, building the castle and assembling her army had taken more time than she had expected. Her command of coercion and antigravity spells was sketchy at the start. But she learned from her mistakes, and she refused to settle for less than what she wanted.

Thus, on the eve of her seventeenth birthday she had more than candles to ignite. She had cannons.

Her pirate fixation had developed gradually. She'd never given much thought to the silly romances shared by her friends in grade school, children who had been led to believe that all pirates were like Disney's Jack Sparrow—cute and essentially harmless. Eva had a different model in mind. She had no desire to be wooed by some smooth-talking swashbuckler. She had contempt for most men, and the few she respected didn't stir anything inside her. She'd read about romance but so far had found little to convince her that it was anything more than another foolish myth. She knew she was attractive, and her magic could compel any man to do her bidding. But she quickly discovered that magic was no help when it came to finding a quality man. The boys and men she'd met so far fell roughly into two categories: those who thought they were strong enough to dominate her and couldn't handle it when they discovered they weren't, and those who were so cowed by her power and beauty that they couldn't perform with conviction even when she offered herself to them.

It would have been totally frustrating had she been looking for love. But as it happened, she didn't think much of love. As far as she could tell from her own life and her mother's example, love was a shabby illusion that didn't last long enough to be worth the effort.

She got through her occasional bouts of loneliness with the unwavering affection Mudley gave her. It was enough, she thought. She lacked for nothing.

Yet as she contemplated her pirate fleet, she couldn't deny that she was looking forward to this next adventure. Much as she had enjoyed the experience of sending forth her ships to pillage and plunder, and seeing the treasures they brought back to her, she was excited by her decision to go along with them on the next voyage. She had never been on a ship of any kind.

Her two closest advisors, the wizard Melinor and the seer Truban, both "on loan" from Magda, had tried to discourage her from going. She chafed at their continual advice and mealy-mouthed suggestions. She knew they took orders from Magda. They warned of seasickness, of the brutality of pirate life, of the vagaries of ocean currents and unpredictable storms. Eva's eyes only glittered brighter.

She was not a little girl anymore. She was a sorceress, the equal of any who might challenge her, and certainly capable of controlling a few hundred simple pirates. If they were foolish enough to test her, they would soon regret it.

A light knock sounded on her chamber door.

"Come," she said.

Elfine, the youngest of her chamber maids, entered and bowed. "Highness, there is a young man to see you."

"Who is he and what does he want?"

"He claims to be an old friend. His name is Clayton. He says he wants to offer his services to you."

The name fell flat on Eva's ear, though something stirred beyond memory's reach. She frowned slightly and said, "Show him in."

He entered the room as if it were his, without hesitation, without drama. He was lean and slightly taller than Eva. A trace of beard outlined his chin; auburn hair framed his face. A guitar was strapped across his back. He stood before her, waiting.

She stared at his face, trying to place him. As he seemed to be waiting for her to speak first, she said, "Do I know you?"

"We've met before. I don't expect you remember me. You've changed since you were in Missouri."

A light came into Eva's eyes. "Clayton. How did you find me?"

"There's a lot of talk about you. Out on the roads. You build a big castle, hire an army, people notice."

"So, you came here because..."

"Seemed like something to do. It was that or go to New York. But I've heard the city's not what it was."

"Nothing is."

"Right." He glanced around at the chamber, with its high ceiling, grand windows and massive fireplace. "This is nice," he said.

"Thanks. Just a little something I threw together."

He looked at her for a moment. "So. You're a sorceress now."

"Yup."

"How's that working out for you?"

"It's pretty cool."

Clayton nodded. "What's your plan?"

"What do you mean?"

"Your agenda. Are you going to take over the world or just lay back and throw parties? Are you going to use your power for good?"

"Good is relative."

"No it's not."

Eva felt the coolness in his tone and had a sudden recollection of Clayton's past. She'd forgotten how serious he was.

"No. You're right," she said. "But it's a big world. I don't think I can fix the whole thing."

Clayton stared at her with an expression she couldn't read.

She shifted in her chair. "What brings you here?" she asked.

"I'm looking for a job. Do you have a musician?"

"Since when are you a musician?"

"Since you turned into a sorceress." His eyes held hers with an unspoken challenge. "Music is a kind of magic."

She smiled slightly. "Are you that good?"

He took his guitar off his back and strummed it. "Shall I play you a song?"

She shrugged. "Sure."

He began to play a melody, adding his voice after a few measures. It was something about a search for truth and beauty. Eva found her attention wandering away from the words. The music was pleasant enough. But what held her rapt was the sight of his fingers moving along the neck of the guitar, the way his head bent to be closer to the strings, the way his hair fell across his cheekbone.

Her heart began to race, and she flushed in surprise at herself. She hadn't felt anything remotely like desire since her last ill-considered flirtation wth one of the captains of her guards. That idiot had fancied himself quite a catch, even for a self-made queen, but his skills in the bedroom were as dull as his conversation, and Eva vowed afterwards that she would rather sleep alone than waste her time with some bore.

Now, however, with his music in her ears and his eyelashes setting her pulse skipping, this young boy had awakened a desire she'd thought was gone for good. *How awkward. I wonder if he even thinks of me that way.*

The idea of seducing him occurred to her. But something made her hesitate. She realized suddenly, as he finished the song and turned his clear eyes upon her, that what she wanted was his respect.

"Thank you," she said. "I haven't heard anyone play like that in a long time. You're very good."

"Thanks." He stood there, as if waiting for her to make the next move.

She fidgeted irritably, almost wishing he would say something to stop her from making a mistake.

"Did you ever find your father?"

Eva frowned. No one in the castle knew anything about her real history. She liked it that way.

"Yes, I did."

"Was he glad to see you?"

"It didn't turn out the way I thought it would."

"Sorry."

"It's okay. I'm glad I did it. I learned some things."

"That can be good."

She smiled. "How about you? What made you decide to become a musician?"

"Oh, you know. The usual. Sex, drugs and money."

She laughed. "And you'd give all that up to work for me?"

He waited half a beat before replying. "I don't need the drugs or money."

And there it was. The heat spreading from her hips to her heart.

"Well. Okay. You drive a hard bargain. I hope."

He laughed. She smiled.

"Would you like something to eat?" she asked.

He grinned.

She shook her head. "And here I thought you were going to be all serious and mature."

"I am. Totally serious." He closed the distance between them, holding the guitar in his right hand, reaching for her with his left.

She grabbed his hand and said, "Let's go get some dinner and I'll tell you about my pirates."

Clayton pulled away slightly and said, "Pirates? That's a joke, right?"

"No. I've got pirates."

"What do you mean by pirates?"

"What does anyone mean by pirates? I mean swords, parrots, swashbuckles. The whole enchilada."

Clayton stared at her, not amused. "Real pirates aren't a joke. They murder people. They rape women."

Eva dropped his hand and shook her head. "Not my pirates. Mine go sailing around looking for buried treasure. Or unburied—they're not choosy. They take things that look useful and bring them back to me. They're not allowed to rape anyone. My pirates like to swagger, but really, they're more Robin Hood than Bluebeard. We take swag from billionaires."

"And what do you do with it?"

She shrugged. "Why do you ask? What do you care?"

"I care because you obviously have a lot of power and resources, and you could be helping people instead of just... Whatever it is you do here."

"Well thanks for the advice. I guess you know all about helping people since you write all those songs to change the world."

Clayton's eyes narrowed.

Eva stepped back and glanced out the window at the light casting a pink glow on the evening clouds. "Listen, if you want to argue, maybe you should just go now. I'm hungry. I'm going to have dinner. You can join me if you want. If you don't, that's your choice."

She started for the door.

He hesitated only a moment before he followed her out.

Chapter 16

The pirates were getting restless.

Cooped up on their ships for weeks, forced to remain anchored in sight of the castle for months, they were starting to question their purpose in life. And worse, they were running low on beer.

"If she's coming, she better come soon, is all I can say." Greg the Destroyer shuffled the deck and dealt another hand.

"What's your rush? This ain't so bad. We got food, beer, women if we want 'em. Might as well enjoy it, I say." Alvin the Bear gathered his cards and rested his meaty forearms on his bulging belly.

"He's right, you know," said Whisker Tom, known more for his bright orange beard than for any particular skill. Tom's career as a mid-level paper-pusher vanished after the Greening. His wife left him to join a band of gypsies, who, like the How Now Cowboys out west, were enjoying a renaissance of sorts since the breakdown of the rule of law. Tom had been drifting, living from hand-to-mouth, when he heard about Eva's pirate project. He jumped at the chance, grew a beard, and got a ring in his ear. He was happier than he'd ever been in his life.

"I heard we're going down to the Caribbean," said Murph, a nervous looking former physics teacher whose school had gone up in smoke during the first wave of riots. He threw down his hand in disgust. "We shouldn't be going anywhere near the tropics at this time of year."

"You worry too much," said Alvin, gathering in the cards.

While Alvin shuffled and dealt the next hand, Murph pursed his lips and glanced up at the clouds. They were puffy as marshmallows, massing on the horizon. The air was calm and warm, the glaze of summer still in the air, though it was almost October. Hurricanes rarely happened up here on the river. But if they headed out to the open seas...

Murph tried to focus on his cards. His eyebrows lifted in stunned surmise as first one, then another, another, and a fourth sly queen peeked at him. Another man might have seen it as an omen of great good fortune.

The other men whistled and hooted in disbelief when Murph laid down his cards.

"See? I told you, you worry too much. You've got luck on your side," said Alvin, slapping Murph on the back.

Murph frowned moodily. "There's no such thing as luck," he said.

***

When at last Eva came on board to take command of her fleet, it was almost Halloween. Her dalliance with Clayton had been diverting for a few weeks, but his unbending moral tone grated on her nerves. She grew weary of his lectures about how she should use her gifts to help humankind.

"Humankind can help itself," she argued. "They always have. They don't need me, and I don't need them."

Although she had delighted in Clayton's passion and his sensitivity to her desires, she decided not to risk ruining it by bringing him on her maiden pirate expedition. Instead she left him in charge of the castle. There were other people who could have done the job, but she thought it might keep him from disappearing while she was away, and perhaps a taste of power would toughen him up. Besides, she couldn't take Mudley on the ship. He had already demonstrated a tendency to seasickness. So, leaving behind her faithful dog and her frisky lover, Eva took to the high seas in search of adventure.

Although the weather was fine during the first two weeks, and they made good progress, once the initial elation wore off she found the hours long and monotonous. The few times they came across a ship worth robbing, the experience had been less than thrilling. Jewelry and priceless antiques meant nothing to

Eva. And the people from whom they liberated such bounty were so pitifully grateful simply to be spared that there wasn't much in the way of pirating drama. After one particularly unsatisfying encounter Eva stared out at the sea, trying to ignore her growing sense of disenchantment. Turning her head, she noticed one of the older pirates watching her with a bemused expression.

"What are you looking at?" she said.

"You tell me," he said.

Eva tapped her foot irritably. "Is that the way you talk to your Queen?"

"Since when are you royalty?"

She glowered at him. "What's your name?"

"Hey You."

Eva rolled her eyes. "Give me a break," she snapped. "I just don't...it doesn't..." She sighed and began again. "I thought it would be more...I don't know. Exciting."

The pirate shrugged. "It's just highway robbery without the highway. It is what it is."

"Is it fun for you?" she asked.

He shrugged again. "It passes the time. It's something to do." He shook his head. "It's all just getting by. Day to day. For us as weren't born with a magic spoon."

"Huh." Eva looked at him more carefully. His head was wrapped in a bandana. A gold hoop hung from one ear. His mahogany skin was creased and pleated from the sun. His eyes were paler than the sky, and fixed upon her with something that almost looked like pity. "Well, if you don't like it, why are you here?"

The pirate grinned. "I could ask the same of you."

"This is my first voyage. You look like you've been around the world a few times."

The sailor nodded. "A few."

"So," she persisted, "why do you keep doing it?"

The sailor glanced out at the sea. "Who knows why we do the things we do? Desire is a mystery." He turned his gaze back to Eva and said, "The only thing worse than never getting what you desire is getting it."

"Why?"

"There's nothing to live for afterwards."

"That's stupid," Eva said. "I would just desire something else."

"Exactly," he said. With that, he stood up, offered her a slight bow, and walked away.

***

For days and days Eva had nothing to do but stare at the horizon. Clouds came and went. Breezes blew or not. The ship creaked and rolled. The men treated her with deference, but mostly ignored her. She chose not to eat with them, preferring to maintain the barrier of rank and privilege. She almost wished she'd brought Clayton along after all. But when she thought of him she inevitably remembered their last conversation, which was more of an argument than a fond farewell.

"Why do you want to do this?" he had said.

"Why shouldn't I do this? It will be fun. An adventure. I'll bring back treasure."

"You have everything you need and more. There are people starving not a mile from here. You could feed them if you would. How can you enjoy all of this while you know other people are suffering?"

"Oh, give it a rest. I'm leaving tomorrow. Can't we talk about something else?" She had reached for him then, hoping that his desire for her would trump his judgment. But he had looked at her with such disappointment that she grew angry and accused him of being a hypocrite.

"I don't see you out there helping the homeless. You think your sappy songs are going to change the world? Get real. The world doesn't change. It's cold and cruel and only the strong survive. It's not fair but that's how it is." She glared at him, surprised at how angry she felt.

"Maybe I should leave now."

"No! You have to stay here and take care of this place while I'm gone."

"You don't need me to do that. Maybe it would be better if I went away."

"When I want you to leave I'll let you know. Until then, you do as I command."

He snorted softly. "Really? You're commanding me now?"

"Just stop being such a jerk, okay? I just want to do this one little pirate adventure. Then you and I can save all the children and puppies and put everything back the way it was in the good old days."

He stared at her for a moment. "They weren't that good."

"I know! That's my point."

He shook his head and looked away. "I'll stay till you get back."

Later, as she gazed out at the cold gray surface of the river, Eva shuddered and wrapped her coat tighter around herself. She couldn't wait to get to the warmer waters down south. In her dreams she sat beneath palm trees and felt sand between her toes.

***

The first thunderhead poked its bruised brow over the horizon as the ships sailed into the azure waters south of St. Martin. The cloud was so far away, it could have been mistaken for a volcanic isle. But within hours the lone cloud had invited a crowd of dark and brooding friends, who rumbled and burst like poison popcorn as they grew larger and swelled higher. The wind turned cold and the sails began to snap and shudder. The color of the sea went from clear, bluish green to gunmetal gray.

Eva stepped out onto the deck and watched the storm approach. It filled her with an exhilarating apprehension. She had imagined that she would be nervous, but she'd never experienced a storm at sea, and she thrilled to the sense of power in the rush of the wind, the crash of the waves against the hull. She could hear the tension in the captain's voice as the crew lowered the sails and braced to ride out the storm.

When he came up to her and advised her to go below until the storm passed, she said she wanted to stay on deck to watch. The four ships were careening wildly in the boiling waves, while the crews tried to maintain a safe distance to avoid crashing into each other. Soaked to the skin and electrified by the wild swoop and swing of the ship rising thirty feet on one wave before plummeting in the trough behind it, Eva had never felt so alive.

The captain, struggling to get close enough to be heard on the tilting wet deck, urged, "Your Grace, it's too dangerous. You must get below."

"Nonsense. My place is here. I'll be fine," she shouted, to be heard above the gale.

The captain opened his mouth to argue, but a huge wave vaulted over the railing and knocked him to the deck. Eva nearly lost her grip on the line that kept her secure in her spot, but the close call didn't scare her so much as convince her she had nothing to fear as long as she held on.

In a way, this was true. Unfortunately, the girl queen had vastly underestimated her opponent.

The snarling winds sucked at the sea, pulling it hundreds of feet into the air, twirling it into typhoon twists that danced madly around the heaving boats. The clouds exploded like bombs. Eva's chest clamped shut with fear at last as the storm snapped two of her ships in half and they vanished under the black waves.

"Is there nothing you can do?" the captain yelled at her, when the mast cracked and crashed to the deck.

"It's too much!" she screamed. And then there was only darkness and roaring water as the ship broke apart and the ocean swallowed it.

Sinking into the darkness she felt a strange presence in the water, as if it were reaching inside her to erase her soul. She opened her mouth to scream but the water rushed in, filling her lungs. As she lost consciousness she sensed a female spirit gathering her, pulling her close.

***

A nibbling at her fingers tickled her toward consciousness. In the twilight space between death and life she dreamed it was Mudley, licking her hand, nudging her to look at him. Her eyelids felt so heavy. She was so tired. Too tired to open her eyes. And besides, she was dead, wasn't she? She tried to remember. She had been on the boat. And then... Her eyes flew open as the memory hit her. She sat up quickly, gasping for breath, and blinking in confusion.

"Ah. She wakes at last," said a female voice.

"Not dead after all," added a different female voice.

Eva squinted and tried to focus. She was in a snug, dimly lit room. It was rocking just enough to tell her she was on a boat. It was not hers.

The sailors gathered around her were dressed in men's garb, but they appeared to be mostly women.

One leaned closer to her and looked her in the eye. "You're a lucky girl," the sailor said.

"Where am I?"

"You're aboard the good ship FaldeRal, in the Caribbean Sea."

"I thought I was dead."

The sailor smiled. "You looked it. We almost didn't bother, but Jan here wanted your sword, so we figured we'd pull you in and go through your pockets anyway."

Eva frowned. "I didn't have a sword."

"That's right. That thing you had strapped to your belt was something else. If I had to guess I'd say it was a wand. Now why would a girl like you be carrying around a wand? Don't tell me you're one of those wanna-be witches, or we might have to throw you back. We don't hold with magic on this ship."

Eva bit her tongue and wondered where they had put her wand. Without it she would have trouble overcoming a crew of sailors, women or not. She tried to keep her face blank as she said, "I'm not a witch. It's not a magic wand. It's a keepsake from my grandmother. She gave it to me for good luck. When I left home."

The sailor, a heavy-set redhead with hoops in her ears and a scar running across her right cheek, studied her for a moment. "Is that right? Well, I guess that explains how you were still alive, floating unconscious in the ocean after a storm like that. We saw it from miles away. Never thought to find any survivors. Didn't think there'd be any ships foolish enough to get caught in something that big. What kind of ship were you on?"

Eva shrugged. "I don't know anything about boats. I was just a passenger. Going to visit my aunt in St. Martin."

"Oh really? And what's her name?"

Eva squirmed irritably. "Maria Carter," she said.

"And what's your name?" the captain asked.

"Angela. Angela Carter."

"I see. Well, Angela, I'm the captain of this ship, and we're not headed anywhere near St. Martin right now, so you can work for your keep until we get someplace we can set you ashore."

"Where are we now?" Eva asked.

"We're headed for Tortuga. After that, Panama. After that...we'll see."

Eva wondered how she long it would take to find her wand, and how many sailors she'd have to kill to get it.

"Mona, take Angela and introduce her to Bets. She might as well start off in the galley. I imagine you're hungry. You've been out cold for three days." She grinned at Eva. "You can work your way up if you stay long enough."

Eva nodded. She had no intention of working her way anywhere. She paused to glance out a porthole and noticed it was raining. She turned to the captain, and asked as casually as she could, "Can I have my wand back?"

The captain gave her a look. "We'll see."

In the galley, the scent of fish stew hung in the dank air, touching off a quick spasm of hunger in Eva's belly, followed closely by a wave of nausea. She felt almost too weak to walk.

The galley occupied one end of the lower deck. Fitted out with chicken coops, an iron stove and a glittering array of knives, the space was dark and hot. A lumpen shape loomed over one counter, muttering or singing, Eva couldn't tell which. The shape turned and fixed her with an orange glare.

"What's this? You want me to cook that for dinner? Hardly worth skinning."

Eva cringed in spite of herself. The woman's jowls quivered like Jello in an earthquake. Her arms were bloated and red; sweat seeped from the black bandana tied over her white hair.

"Cap'n says she's to work for you," said Mona, giving Eva a shove before leaving her alone with the cook.

The cook put one fist on her hip and looked Eva up and down. "Can you cook?"

Eva swallowed. "Yes."

The cook snorted. "We'll see about that. You hungry?"

Eva nodded.

The cook pointed to the chicken cages and said, "Kill two of those and pluck 'em."

Eva scowled but did as she was told. Until she got her strength back and recovered her wand she would have to play dumb. She quickly wrung the necks of the chickens and set to work stripping them of feathers. *I'm alive*, she told herself. That was a start.

The cook worked steadily, silent but for her snatches of song and mutterings to herself. As soon as Eva finished one task, the woman gave her another order. When the meal was prepared, the cook rang a bell and the crew clattered down the stairs and filled the benches on either side of the long table. Eva didn't see a place to sit.

The cook nudged her with an elbow and pointed to a barrel by the sink, "Serve the crew, then you can eat."

After Eva finished serving the sailors, she ladled a portion into a bowl and sat on the barrel to eat it. She had never tasted anything better. The cook passed out hard bread to sop up the stew, and tossed a chunk to Eva. The sailors ignored her while they ate. She studied them, finding no common denominator, other than gender. They were dressed like college kids Eva remembered seeing back in Washington. Jeans and T-shirts, lots of tattoos and ear candy. They were all browned and looked fit, at least compared to the cook, whose obesity would have made climbing any mast a challenge. They seemed carefree and congenial. Eva wondered if there were any men on the ship, and if their absence had something to do with the mood.

"Hey, little girl, where you from?"

She started at being addressed. They'd been ignoring her presence so completely she'd almost forgotten they could see her.

"North Carolina," she said, without thinking, and instantly realized she should have been working on her backstory.

"Whereabouts in North Carolina? I'm from Raleigh," said a blonde sailor with a pixie cut.

"My family's from Wilmington," Eva said smoothly, picking a town she had been to a few times as a kid.

The sailor shot a look across the table, and Eva felt a shift in the room, as if everyone at the table had inhaled at the same time. She turned to the captain and caught a flicker of pity in her eyes.

No one spoke for a moment. Then the captain lifted her chin and asked, "So, all your family's from Wilmington?"

Eva frowned. "No. Just most of them. Why?"

"Ain't no Wilmington anymore," growled a pinch-faced sailor at the end of the table.

"Shut up, Bridge. We don't know that for certain." The captain looked at Eva as she said this.

"What do you mean?" Eva asked.

"We don't stay in contact with the outside much, but we've been hearing reports on the radio. Since the storm. Sounds like it was bigger than anyone knew. A lot bigger."

Eva's throat tightened. She didn't know a soul in Wilmington, but if other coastal towns had been damaged...

"How much bigger? Wilmington's far away from here, isn't it?"

"So's New York," mumbled the one they called Bridge.

"The storm hit New York?"

The captain looked around the table. "The truth is, we don't know how big the storm was. Or if it was a storm at all. It's still raining, case you haven't noticed." She turned to a skinny, sallow young sailor sitting apart from the rest. "JayPeg, tell them what you told me."

JayPeg swallowed the bite she was chewing, and said, "It's hard to know if any of it's true. Sounds too crazy." She shrugged. "But it's not good. There's some saying it's the apocalypse."

"Again? Didn't we already have that?" said Bridge.

A murmur of agreement ran through the crew. "Quiet," the captain said. Then she turned back to JayPeg and said, "Explain."

"There's a lot of talk about storms. Not just here. Off the coast of Africa. The English Channel. Lot of ships lost. There's a rumor going around that Florida is gone."

"What?" said the captain.

"That's what they're saying."

"Who's they?"

"I don't know. People with radios. People who've been living on their boats ever since the Greening, waiting for this. Expecting, you know, the end of everything."

"That's crazy," said Eva.

JayPeg shrugged. "Maybe it is. Maybe it isn't. All I know is, we haven't sighted any land since that so-called storm started. Until we do, I wouldn't rule anything out."

The room went silent but for the sound of the rain pounding the deck above them.

After a moment the captain stretched her arms above her head and said, "Well. No point in worrying. Once the rain stops, if it turns out it's the end of the world, we'll figure something out. Long as there are still fish in the sea, we'll get by."

"But what about when we die?" asked a sailor with grizzled gray hair and yellow teeth.

"Well Cynthia, we're all going to die eventually. This way we won't be missing anything after we're gone." The captain smiled sweetly and a ripple of laughter went around the room.

The sailors finished eating, and most went back on deck. Eva remained fixed at the table, stunned into silence.

"Hey," Bets barked, nudging her out of her trance. "These pots ain't gonna wash themselves."

Eva was too lost in thought to argue. She wondered if any of it was true, or if the sailors were messing with her. But they had seemed genuinely surprised too. She wished she could believe they were teasing her. But even as she thought back to the nightmarish memory of her ship breaking apart and the waves engulfing her, she realized with a sick horror that the worst might be yet to come.

CHAPTER 17

A few days earlier Shiloh was straining to keep the binoculars focused on a pair of scarlet dragons flying ahead of black storm clouds.

Swooping across the sky, carving evasive patterns on the wind, the dragons were closing in on a small band of prairie outlaws armed with rocket launchers. The outlaws fired another off-target shot at the dragons and whooped with frustration or glee. At this distance Shiloh couldn't really tell which, but she had no intention of getting any closer to those idiots. Neither they nor the dragons had taken any notice of her, and she planned to keep it that way.

She took careful aim with her SpellNet and gently placed her finger on the trigger, holding her breath as she waited for the perfect moment. A cold wet drop splatted on her neck. She frowned and looked up.

The storm clouds had dropped so low they choked the daylight out of the sky. Another cold drop landed in her eye. She shook her head to clear her vision, and in that instant caught a glimpse of the dragons, streaking away from the oncoming storm like a pair of red rockets, smoke—or was it steam?—trailing behind them.

It wasn't like dragons to break off an attack. Shiloh looked back at the outlaws, who were scattering like ants abandoning a flooded nest. There was smoke or steam hissing off them too.

She had little time to puzzle over this, because at that moment the wall of clouds cracked open with volcanic power, and water took over the world.

She tried to see where the outlaws had gone, but the rain was so heavy she could hardly see her own feet as she struggled to find her way back to the vent. She'd get back to the outlaws later.

Trudging across the slippery Kansas field, she looked for the small grove of stunted oak trees that she had seen right after she vented to the area. In the darkness of the deluge she would be lucky to find it. She wondered if she should just hunker down and wait for the storm to pass, but another glance at the angry sky was enough to convince her to keep walking.

By the time she stumbled into the airless murk of the vent zone she was exhausted from pushing against the wind and rain. She trudged through the zone, slipping out when she got to the vent at P Street. Any hope she'd had that the weather would be better in D.C. vanished instantly.

If she hadn't recognized the brick sidewalks and gingko trees she might have thought she'd made a wrong turn and arrived back in Kansas. The rain hammered down with machine-like intensity. There was something unnatural about it that chilled Shiloh to the bone.

When she reached the townhouse she dropped her equipment on the floor, and slipped upstairs to get into some dry clothes.

Josh called up to her from the kitchen. "Are you okay? I didn't expect you back so soon."

"I'm fine," she yelled through the bathroom door.

As she toweled off she glanced over her shoulder at her reflection in the mirror and did a double take. She looked down at her bicep and frowned. She turned around and checked her other bicep, thinking perhaps in her wet confusion she'd gotten turned around in the mirror. But the mirror didn't change its story. Her tattoo was gone.

She stood stunned, trying to remember if she'd seen it in the morning. She was sure she had. After seventeen years it was as much a part of her as the gap between her front teeth or the mole on her throat. She leaned against the bathroom wall and tried not to panic. If the tattoo was gone, would her connection to Deep Magic be gone as well?

Reflexively she reached for the Hexcaliber around her neck. It was cool against her skin, but that didn't mean much in the house. She seldom encountered people infected with Deep Magic in Washington.

She finished dressing and went downstairs.

Josh had poured her a glass of wine. She could tell he was in a good mood, glad that she was home early. It had been a while since they had enjoyed the luxury of several days and nights together. The simplest things—doing laundry, making pancakes, going for a walk—seemed deliciously self-indulgent.

When she took the glass from him, he saw her face and immediately asked, "What's wrong?"

"I don't know. Maybe nothing. It's just... I'm a little freaked out because my tattoo is gone."

"Your tattoo? *The* tattoo?"

"Yeah. I don't have any others."

"When did this happen? How could it..."

"I don't know. I mean, I guess if Jack's still got me on his radar, he could have done it. But why would he? If he even could from there." She sat down on the couch and took a sip of wine. "I'd rather not think he's over here."

Josh sat next to her and kissed her cheek. "Hey. Maybe it's nothing to worry about. Maybe it was designed to disappear after a certain length of time."

Shiloh stared across the room, lost in a memory. She could still recall that strange tingling burn when, with a flick of his fingers, Jack had infused her blood with ancient magic. It had seemed impossible and a little frightening at the time, but after all these years she had come to depend on her ability to summon energy from the magic in her veins. Now suddenly it was gone. She sat up straighter.

"Maybe the tattoo isn't necessary anymore. Maybe it fades once you really possess the skills," she mused.

Josh shrugged. "How can you know?"

"Good question. I sure don't want to go out and try to take down some demon and find out then that my mojo's gone. I need to do some tests."

Josh put his arm around her and squeezed gently. "Can it wait till tomorrow?"

She tried to return his smile, though in truth she was more rattled than she wanted to admit. "Sure. Maybe I'm just worried over nothing. Maybe it will be back tomorrow. That rain is crazy. It was raining in Kansas too. Maybe my skin kind of went into shock."

"Well, you're safe now. And you don't have to go out into it again tonight. The weather man said this rain is going to stick around for a few days."

"Huh," Shiloh said, glancing out at the water streaking down the window. The sky was dark already. The rain slashed against the pane as if it were trying to get inside. Shiloh shivered and leaned closer to Josh. Maybe a few days off would be nice.

The next morning the rain was still thrumming on the roof. Shiloh and Josh spent the day playing house. She dug out some of her mother's recipes to use for their Thanksgiving dinner. They watched the daily newscast and learned that the torrential rain wasn't limited to the Washington area. It wasn't only nationwide either. If the reports could be believed, it was raining in Europe, Africa, South America, even in Australia.

Shiloh looked at Josh as they sat absorbing the reports. He didn't say anything. They both avoided talking about the weather after that.

On Thanksgiving she cooked the turkey. They ate pie and potatoes and drank wine. And listened to the rain.

***

Clayton was reaching for Eva in his sleep. Since she had left, his dreams were feverish with longing and so intense that he often awoke more tired than when he had gone to bed. But this night a persistent whimpering worked its way into his dream and filled him with anxiety. He sat up groggily and smelled Mudley, who had taken to sleeping as close to Clayton as he could.

Clayton sighed and reached out to rub the dog's ears, but Mudley seemed more distressed than usual. Clayton sat up straighter and listened in the dark. It was raining, a sound that usually soothed him to sleep. This rain lashed at the windows and banged on the roof. Clayton swung his legs to the side of the bed and stepped into a cold puddle on the floor. He shot an accusing glance at Mudley. But when he lit a candle and looked down he saw that the entire floor was flooded. Eva's bedroom was on the highest floor in one of the castle towers. Clayton frowned and got out of bed to check on the extent of the leak.

His feet squished through something before finding a solid surface. Clayton moved the candle to shine on the floor, expecting to see a soggy rug. But when the light shone on the polished stone floor a sort of rippling effect gave Clayton a momentary flash of vertigo.

"Weird," he muttered.

He stood up carefully. His feet sank slightly into the floor, as if it were wet mud or concrete. Wide awake, he grabbed some clothes and pulled them on quickly. Then he got his guitar and stepped out into the hall. The light was flickering and dim, but even in the wet gloom Clayton could see the walls sliding, oozing downward as the rain worked its way into the castle.

He called Mudley and began to run as fast as he could on the mushy floor. When he reached the guard stationed by the stairs, he told the man to sound the alarm and get everyone out of the castle.

"But sir, it's raining," the guard objected. "And it's the middle of the night."

"Just do it. The castle is dissolving. If it collapses before we get everyone out..."

The guard's eyes went wide as he realized Clayton was serious. He ran to the bell tower and within minutes a piercing clang echoed through the castle. Clayton splashed down the corridors, checking to see that every room was emptied. Many complained, and a few refused to budge until Clayton pulled them to their feet and they sank up to their ankles in magically induced stone that was no longer convinced it wasn't merely sand. Some of the servants argued, insisting it was just a little water. They moved reluctantly and refused to leave without gathering their prized possessions. A few attempted to add some of Eva's bounty to their packs.

Rushing from room to room Clayton shouted, "Come on. You don't have time for this. The whole building is going to collapse."

Some of the staff, seeing his face, dropped their bundles and ran for the gate. Others ignored him. In one room he found a woman methodically wrapping china ware while her infant child wailed in his cot.

"Madame, I'm taking your child to safety," he said, raising his voice to be heard above the lashing rain.

The woman glanced at him and smiled. "Thank you, sir. I'll be right along."

"You have to come now. You'll be buried alive," he shouted.

"Ah, calm yourself. It's just a bit of rain as never hurt anybody. You go along. I'll be able to work faster without Jory bawling at me."

Clayton considered trying to carry her as well as the child, but she was a stout woman, and he suspected she'd struggle. He shook his head, grabbed the baby, and ran out of the room.

As soon as he had cleared the building he handed the child to a woman in the crowd and turned to go back for the mother just as a jagged spear of lightning split the sky and struck the castle like a broad sword going through butter.

The once-solid walls drizzled and melted so fast Clayton couldn't even find the gate. All that was left was a small mountain of wet sand.

Mudley howled at the rain. The people who had escaped stared at the wreckage of Eva's magical structure. But the rain continued without pause, and it was dark and cold. No one hung around for long.

Except for Clayton and Mudley. Clayton found shelter for himself and his guitar under a wagon that had been parked outside the castle. Mudley curled up beside him, and there they waited until dawn while the rain kept falling.

***

After the first week the news stories changed focus from the rain itself to the widespread flooding. The entire state of Florida had been declared a national disaster area. Residents were urged to abandon their homes and head north as fast and as far as possible. This would have been a challenge even before the Greening. Now, with most people reduced to relying on bicycles and horses, the crisis went from dire to desperate in days.

As the second week of nonstop rain pelted Earth, residents in coastal areas began to flee inland. More highways and bridges got washed away; the situation became critical even for those living far from the usual flood-prone areas. Vast portions of the flat Midwest were underwater.

Speculation as to the cause of all this ran the gamut from the scientific to the apocalyptic. Presidents and heads of state around the world called for calm and cooperation, but violence and mayhem swirled in the eddies of the floodwaters.

Shiloh and Josh stayed close to home, rarely leaving the house except to make short trips for such supplies as could be found.

On the night of the eighteenth day of what the media had taken to calling FloodGate, Shiloh was staring numbly at the news broadcast when Josh came in and sat next to her. "Hey,

I've been meaning to ask. Did you get rid of your lizard? Or did it die? I haven't seen it around for a while."

Shiloh looked up with the dazed expression of someone regaining consciousness after a blow to the head. She hadn't thought about the lock-lizard for weeks. A cold premonition took her breath away. She jumped off the couch and ran upstairs.

After a quick search around the bedroom she sat down on the bed and tried to remember the last time she'd seen the little guy. He usually slithered into her backpack when she went out on missions, as if he knew she might need him. Suddenly she remembered her soaked backpack. She hadn't touched it since that first day of rain. She recalled now that Josh had hung it out to dry on the back porch.

She clumped down the stairs and ran to the back door. The backpack was still hanging on the outside knob. She opened the door and grabbed the pack. It wasn't dripping wet anymore, but it wasn't dry either. Rain beat ceaselessly on the tin roof and blew in through the screens. She closed the door and carried the backpack into the kitchen. With a sinking heart she opened it. An orange coating of rust completely covered the cold lock. She took it out and tried to wipe off the rust with a dish towel. Maybe the lizard had slept through the whole thing, she speculated feverishly. But the more she tried to clean up the antique lock, the less hopeful she felt. The lock was rusted solid. She wondered if the lizard had died, or if he was trapped inside. Either way, she felt a hurt made more bitter by the sting of guilt. She'd completely forgotten the lock-lizard. She had taken him for granted for years, just like her tattoo. And now he was gone too. Was it coincidence, or something else?

Josh was quiet, sensing her mood. She put the rusty lock on top of her bureau, nestling it in a hand towel, in case the lock-lizard somehow transformed. Shiloh couldn't help hoping the warmth of the room might bring him back, even though she had begun to suspect that this change was linked to others.

For instance, in all the news coverage since the deluge began, there had been no reports of magic-induced violence, no gangs of self-made trolls running amok looting, no dragon sightings. Josh hadn't encountered a single paranormal report on his regular internet monitoring. Shiloh and Josh had both enjoyed the initial relief of this hiatus, but as the rain-related devastation mounted they began to wonder if the rain itself was evidence of some fresh magical hell.

Thus, on the thirtieth day after it began, when the rains stopped and the sun shone again on the world, Shiloh and Josh were only moderately enthusiastic, waiting for the other rubber boot to drop.

Shiloh gave Josh's hand a squeeze as they prepared to go out the front door.

"Don't worry," he said. "Maybe the worst is over."

She rolled her eyes. "Hold that thought," she said.

Sunlight dazzled on the freshly washed streets. Even the brick sidewalks gleamed. It was chilly, only a few days before Christmas, but there were no decorations anywhere. The incessant rain had dampened what little Christmas spirit remained in the post-Greening world. No one could afford the kind of extravagant displays that had characterized the holiday in the early 21st century. And the freakish growth of vegetation since the Greening had also cast a pall over the tradition of putting up garlands and wreaths. People still put up the occasional Christmas tree, but there had been a marked shift in the popular attitude.

Still, Shiloh felt vaguely puzzled by the appearance of the neighborhood as they walked around on the day the rain stopped. She was trying to put her finger on what was different when she stepped off the curb and slipped on an oil slick. Josh caught her elbow and saved her from landing hard on the pavement.

"Wow. Haven't done that in a while," she said. "Thanks." She smiled at Josh, but he was staring at the pavement. She looked down to see what held his attention.

In the first few years after the Greening many cars were simply left on the street, abandoned by their owners. Some were transformed into planters, some into urban art of sorts. Over time most of them were gradually dismantled and carried off. But a few old vehicles remained exactly where they had been eighteen years earlier when The Greening made them obsolete.

The place where Shiloh slipped was right behind one of these old relics, a once-immaculate Mercedes sedan. Before the rains the car had all but disappeared under its mantle of vines and weeds. Birds had nested in the thick growth covering the car's trunk. Shiloh gasped as she recognized the car. All the foliage and greenery which had cloaked it for years was gone. Covering the car now was an iridescent film of oil, a slithering, rainbow-hued layer oozing onto the pavement.

Shiloh's jaw dropped as she took in the extent of the oil slick. It covered the street, spilled over parts of the sidewalk, pooled up at the corners of every alley.

"Holy crap," she whispered, gazing wide-eyed at Josh.

He looked back at her and said, "Uh oh."

They walked on, carefully avoiding spots where the oil was thick. There were a few other people out on the streets, shaking their heads and whistling in awe. One older man stood in his bathrobe at the end of his driveway smiling gleefully at an opalescent puddle. He beamed at Shiloh and Josh as they walked around the puddle. "Big oil is back, baby!"

Shiloh bit her tongue. They hurried on. "Come on," said Josh. "I need to get online. If this is everywhere..."

Shiloh grabbed his hand and they ran together down the slippery sidewalk.

CHAPTER 18

While the rain continued day after day, the good ship FaldeRal sailed southward.

No one talked about the rain, but the crew kept their eyes on the horizon. They had seen no sign of land since the storm started. The long days began and ended with muttering and rumors. Some said they'd been blown way off course. With radio contact erratic and the stars hidden behind constant clouds, there was no way to verify their position. Some whispered that the world had been wiped clean by the Goddess. Others credited the Devil. Uncertainty hung in the air like the scent of rotten cheese. A few voices dared to suggest turning back. The captain scoffed at this idea.

"What makes anyone think it will be better up north? If there's no one left but us, I'm still captain of this ship. In fact, if there's no one left but us, I just got promoted. I'm Queen of the World. So quit your complaining. If you don't like it on this ship you're welcome to get off."

Eva tuned out the bickering and speculating. She didn't know these women and she didn't plan to spend the rest of her life taking orders from them. Somewhere stashed away on this ship was her wand. If only she could find it.

Knowing that the captain and crew didn't tolerate the use of magic meant nothing to Eva. She had learned how to make reluctant soldiers obey her every whim. Teaching a bunch of female sailors to jump when she told them to couldn't be any more difficult. But considering the odds, she wanted to recover her wand before she made her move.

The size of the ship daunted her, however. Her early attempts to pry a hint out of anyone about the wand's hiding place had been met with swift and firm refusals. And she didn't want the captain to get the idea that the wand was anything more than an object of sentimental value. She even tried crying while telling one of the younger sailors a long complicated lie about how much the wand meant to her, hoping that perhaps someone might feel sympathy for her. The tears backfired. The crew christened her Snivella.

Down in the galley Eva scowled at the small mountain of fish to be cleaned for dinner. Bets was up on deck. She was alone. She wondered if she dared use a simple conjuring to clean the damned fish at least. Why not? She concentrated her mind and focused on her core reserve of Deep Magic. She groped for a moment, like a person in the dark reaching for a light switch in an unfamiliar room.

She broke out in a sweat. Normally she could summon her core magic as easily as making a fist. She tried to relax and let the magic come, the way it always had before. But she felt nothing. No shiver of current, no hiss of energy, no sizzle of light. The fish stared at her with their dead eyes. Eva picked one up and threw it across the room. It landed at the doorway just as Bets arrived.

"Don't play with the food," she snapped, kicking it back to Eva.

Eva scowled and started cleaning the fish.

Later that night, after dinner was over and she was finished for the night, she went up on deck, huddled in the rain where no one could see her, and tried a few simple conjuring experiments. Nothing worked. She couldn't lift a bucket, set fire to a rope. She couldn't even stop a loud-mouthed sailor from talking. It used to be one of her favorite tricks.

She stared out at the gray sea and felt for the first time its vast indifference to her. If she fell in now, she would no doubt drown, and who would care? No one on this ship certainly. She could hear the crew laughing and singing down below. They didn't care about magic. They didn't rely on it. They had each other.

Eva wrapped her arms about her chest and tried to stop the rising tide of doubt. She was alone. Far from anything like home.

She sat down on a barrel and tried to stay calm. Maybe her magic was just on the blink. Maybe being nearly drowned had messed up the works. This idea gave her some comfort. The more she considered it, the more she liked this theory. Maybe she just needed to be patient. She could be patient.

She looked up at the clouds and wondered how far the rising sea had spread. If Florida was really gone, would the Chesapeake Bay be covering miles of lowlands? And what about the Hudson? She thought of her castle, perched high on a cliff above the river. Surely it would be all right. Wouldn't it?

***

As the days stretched into weeks and still no land was sighted, the mood on the ship darkened. The carefree joking and singing grew less frequent, the silences longer. The first mad fever of conjecturing passed, and in its place a kind of grim calm pervaded. The relentless rain played on like a deranged drummer's solo.

Alone with her secret hope, Eva kept apart from the others, and they showed no eagerness to befriend her. A few sailors had already floated the idea that Eva was somehow responsible for the rain. In the long idle hours the need to assign blame festered among the crew, and it came naturally to some to blame bad luck on a stranger too pretty for her own good. Eva heard the whispers. She knew she had enemies. She looked forward to dispatching them as soon as she got her powers back.

But progress on that front was nonexistent. Although she woke each day with hope, the only strength she felt in her body was the gradual development of muscles thanks to the menial labor she was forced to do. Eva began to wonder if even the wand would help, if she ever got it back.

One evening after another meager meal was finished, Eva was sitting on deck welcoming the coolness of the rain on her face when she saw the captain approaching.

The captain stopped beside her. Eva didn't look up. Something clattered to the deck. Her heart leapt at the sight of her wand.

"Here's the deal," the captain said. "If you can find us land with that thing, maybe you can stay on the ship. Otherwise... we're running low on supplies. Unless we find land soon, we'll run out of firewood. We might have to lighten our load."

Eva looked up at the captain. "You're going to throw me off?"

"Not if you find us land."

"What if I can't?"

"Then I guess you can keep your little stick. Maybe it will keep you afloat."

Eva grabbed the wand and closed her eyes, waiting for the rush of energy to fill her veins. She gripped it tighter. Her palm started to sweat. A sickening dread crept into her mind. Her magic spark was dead.

She opened her eyes and stared up at the captain with a look of fear and hate.

"It's not a wand!" she said, jumping to her feet. "It's just the only thing I have left in this world." She gazed around at the crew who had gathered to watch. "You want to blame all of this on me? Go ahead! You think killing me will save you? You're even stupider than I thought."

She faced them all, brandishing the wand like a sword, willing it to become one, something sharp at least so she could take a few them with her when they threw her overboard.

In the charged moment, while the rain drummed on, the captain glanced at the crew. Finally she turned back to Eva and inclined her head slightly. "That'll do for now. Maybe you're telling the truth. Maybe not. I'd be careful about insulting the crew. Patience is a virtue, but we are none of us without sin. Goodnight."

The captain went to back to the helm, while most of the crew shook their heads and walked away. Eva stared out at the dark sea until her eyes burned.

That night she slept with the wand pressed against her skin. She was beginning to think something was really wrong with her magic. She slept badly, her nightmares awash with salty waves.

When the rain finally stopped on the thirtieth day after the storm began, the sun rose like a smile on the horizon. The crew rejoiced, and for a while Eva brightened too in the hope that the return of the sun would restore her power.

She was taking a break on deck after the midday meal, twisting the wand in her hands and imagining the miseries she would inflict on the crew when she got her power back, when a shadow fell across her. She looked up and saw the one they called JayPeg.

"Mind if I sit with you?" she asked.

Eva grunted. "Does it matter?"

JayPeg remained standing, silent.

"Fine. Sit." Eva snapped.

JayPeg slipped to the deck in one fluid motion. She sat with her knees up and wrapped her arms around them. She smiled easily at Eva and said, "How're you doing?"

"Like you care."

JayPeg shook her head and smiled. "Oh come on, kid. Everyone's a little edgy right now. You gotta give 'em a chance. They can't hate you unless you hate yourself."

Eva grunted. "What the hell does that mean? I don't hate myself. They hate me for no reason."

"Are you sure? No offense, kid, but you don't seem like a happy camper."

"Huh. What have I got to be happy about?"

"Well, for starters, you're alive. From where I'm sitting that puts you in a very small and privileged minority. We might be all that's left of humanity."

"Are you trying to cheer me up or get me to kill myself?"

JayPeg laughed. Eva smiled in spite of herself.

"See, there. I wondered what you would look like in a smile," JayPeg said. "It works for you. You should try it more often."

"Why? I'm stuck here on this boat with a bunch of people who hate me, and the world is finished. What I have I got to smile about?"

JayPeg tilted her head. "The thing is, smiles are like magic. They make things happen. They open doors, light up rooms, ease the tightness in your shoulders. All good stuff. Also, the best way to piss off somebody who's bugging you? Smile at them. Works like a charm."

Eva grinned.

JayPeg raised her eyebrows. "Am I bugging you?"

Eva grinned wider. "No. Thanks. Really. You're the first person who's... You know, just talked to me since I got here."

"I know. We're not a very, um, socially evolved group. There's a kind of Darwinian principle at work here. Best way to beat it is to make yourself useful. Better still, indispensable." She paused and gave Eva an appraising look. "Charm can also work, but it's harder to pull off with this bunch."

"Thanks for the tip," Eva said.

"Yeah, well. The captain has to be badass, because, you know, it's a captain thing. She's not gonna throw you off the ship." JayPeg paused and stole a look behind her before she continued. "That's not to say someone else might not try. But, you know. Pirates. What are you gonna do?"

They sat and watched the clouds rolling slowly across the sky.

"Do you really think we're all that's left?" Eva asked.

"Nah. I've seen those computer models of what Earth would look like if all the ice melted, and there's no way water covers the whole planet."

"But, it has before, right? I mean. You know. Supposedly. The Bible, the flood."

"I wouldn't have pegged you for a churchy."

"I'm not. But everybody knows the story."

"Yeah, well, if you remember the punch line, it went something like: 'No more water, the fire next time.' So even if you buy into that sort of thing, this doesn't fit. This," she waved an arm at the vast empty horizon, "is something not on the apocalyptic menu."

"Maybe it's the special."

JayPeg grinned. "You're growing on me, kid."

"So...what's the plan here? Are we going anywhere or just floating around in circles?"

"Shirley hasn't said anything specific, but judging by the wind and waves, it looks like we're sailing on the ocean formerly known as Florida."

"Shirley?"

"That's the captain, to you."

"Really?"

"I wouldn't give it too much thought."

"Shirley. Huh."

"Get over it."

Eva stood up and looked over the railing, peering into the water as if she might be able to see DisneyWorld. "It's hard to believe," she said, after a few minutes.

JayPeg joined her at the rail. "Yeah. But they had to know it was coming."

"Not this fast. Not this sudden," Eva said. "That's why it doesn't fit. It stinks of..."

"Magic, huh?"

"Maybe. Or something like it."

JayPeg nodded and squinted into the sun. "Yeah. But, seems to me, if we keep going northeast, we've got to get to higher ground. And then we'll have a better idea what's going on."

"How long will that take, do you think?"

"Hard to say. I wouldn't be surprised if we started seeing signs in a day or so. There's the Smokies, the whole

Appalachian range. They might look like islands, but they've got to be out there."

***

In the days that followed, Eva continued trying her wand in vain. She kept it sheathed on her belt anyway. At least it served as a reminder of the life she'd had before scrubbing pots and plucking chickens turned her hands rough and red.

There had been no repeat of the conversation with JayPeg, but Eva had stopped brooding and sulking, and as a result she started noticing things on the ship she hadn't bothered with before.

She was enjoying a moment on the deck, watching dolphins slipping by alongside the ship, when she heard a clear soprano voice singing a familiar tune.

Do you love an apple? Do you love a pear?
Do you love a laddy, with curly brown hair?
Oh but still, I love him, I can't deny him
I'll be with him, wherever he goes.

Curious, she ventured closer, and was startled to discover that the singer was the one called Agnes, an older woman who wore a perpetual scowl. She was mending a sail as she sang, her head down, her face glowing with serenity. Eva was still staring at her when she finished the song and looked up. Agnes held her gaze for a long moment, reading Eva's expression.

"Do ya know the song?" she asked, finally.

"Yes. That was beautiful," Eva said.

Agnes nodded. "My mother used to sing it. Makes me think of home."

She turned back to her mending, and Eva went back to the kitchen. But after that, whenever she heard singing, she paused in her chores and tried to get close enough to hear better. Her own mother had never sung to her, but the songs Agnes knew reminded Eva of summer visits at her grandparents' home, where the mountain music seemed woven into the very air. She wondered if that place was underwater now too.

A few days later loud shouts erupted at dawn. Eva ran up on deck where the rest of the crew crowded at the rail, pointing across the water to a smudge on the horizon.

She pushed in next to JayPeg and asked, "Is it land?"

JayPeg shrugged. "It's something. We won't know until we get closer."

Speculation ran wild as the ship sped over the waves.

"Could be a wreck."

"Might be a pirate gang."

"Maybe what's left of Tampa."

The captain kept silent until they got close enough to discern the tops of the trees. "Can't tell what kind of trees they are. And looks like they go on for a ways. We'll have to watch that we don't get snagged on others we can't see."

As they came within a mile or so of the trees, they began to see other things floating in the water—trunks and branches, clusters of junk, old boards and such tangled with seaweed and trash. In the shallows as they came closer they saw other trees under the water; ahead, the land from which the trees rose extended into the distance, dotted with pines and tall oaks draped with swaying curtains of gray moss.

At first glance it didn't appear there was anywhere to dock the ship, nor much reason to do so. A source for fresh water and fire wood would be enough.

The captain looked around at the crew, none of whom appeared particularly eager to set off into the tangled swamp. "Any volunteers?" she asked.

Eva leapt up and said, "Let me go."

The captain glanced at her with some impatience. "Give me one good reason."

Eva's heart was racing. She had no logical reason. "I'm younger than the rest of the crew. I've got better ears. And I'm from the South. I know this country. I can see things and hear things. I can be useful. Please. I want to be useful. I'm not just a chicken plucker."

The captain eyed her steadily.

"You're not afraid of alligators?"

Eva held her tongue. She hadn't given alligators a thought, though now that she did, she wasn't too keen on the idea. But it didn't matter. Something raw and real was pulsing through her body. She didn't know why or how, but she was convinced that she should be part of the exploring party. And if a chance to escape came along, well, she wouldn't mind.

"Anyone else dying for a chance to be alligator bait?" the captain asked.

Karin Stephenson, a tall young woman from Boston who had formerly competed on a crew team, raised her hand without hesitation.

Sheila Barnes, known as Barny, one of the captain's inner circle, stepped forward. Agnes moved into place beside her.

"Are you sure, Aggie?" the captain asked. "It might not be a pleasure cruise."

"It'll be a change. I could use one," said the older woman.

When no one else volunteered, the captain looked back at Eva. "Fine. You go. But don't get any stupid ideas out there, understand? If you do, the alligators won't be your worst problem."

They set off in a dinghy. Eva sat in the prow and strained to see into the swamp ahead. A heron flapped its broad wings above them, beating a quiet rhythm in the still air. Eva watched, trying to see where it landed, but it disappeared in the distance, still flapping. As they approached the swamp, the color of the water took on a deeper hue. By the time they reached the gray trunks, the water was dark as pitch.

The air hummed with insects. The scent of algae mixed with pine sap filled Eva's nose. She nearly choked on the pollen and mosquitoes. A turtle slipped noiselessly into the water as they navigated past a barricade of fallen limbs and trunks. Vines coiled like snakes around the slippery trees, and more than once Eva thought she saw one move. She sat rigid, her eyes scanning the oily water for alligators. The lagoon seemed to go on forever.

Stealing a glance behind them, Eva nearly let out a shriek when a dangling vine like a cold wet finger brushed against her neck. When she realized she'd lost sight of where they had entered the swamp, a clammy fear took hold of her.

"Stop," she said, quietly.

The sailors stopped rowing, and the silence grew thicker. Eva had a feeling that she was missing some important clue. She held her breath and slowly peered into the watery woods surrounding them.

"What is it?" Barny whispered.

Eva put a finger to her lips and looked up into the canopy of vines and leaves. She closed her eyes and focused with her mind, listening for the slightest breath. A minute later she sat back and opened her eyes.

"There's something up there," she whispered.

They waited another silent minute. Barny shook her head and said, "Come on. I'm not going up there. Unless you are, we're moving on."

They continued working their way through the trees, but the gaps were getting tighter and the water was getting shallower. When one of the oars got hung up on a branch just below the surface, they stopped and Barny looked ahead.

"Well, children, I guess this is where we take a little hike."

"Ugh," said Eva, frowning into the black water. "What about the gators?"

"You've got a knife, right?"

"Um, no."

"You can just shove your magic stick down its throat," Karin suggested.

Eva frowned and glanced up into the trees again. She hadn't heard or seen anything, but her skin was crawling with the sense that they were being watched.

They tied the boat to a tree and squelched off in the direction that seemed to lead to firmer ground. Eva's boots weren't tall enough. Within minutes they were thoroughly wet inside. She hoped they might at least slow down an alligator's teeth.

Their progress was slow and noisy with the splashing, sucking sounds of their boots being pulled out of the ooze. They began to see clumps of sea grasses and ferns, scraggly bushes and scrawny pines clinging to sandy spots above the water. Sunlight fell in slanting bars between the cypress trees. Eva heard a shrill cry and looked up to see a big osprey flying overhead with a fish in its talons.

They had been slogging ahead for a while when Eva stumbled over a fallen tree and fell into a thicket of brambles and vines. She heard the sailors laughing as she sat up to examine the scratches on her legs. Something prickled under her skin. She lifted her eyes and stared into the bushes. A pair of pale blue eyes stared back.

Eva held her breath. The girl looked to be maybe six or seven years old, scrawny and fierce. Her skin was the color of caramel, her face small and elfin. Eva took a quick look at her ears just to be on the safe side. Pointless.

"Don't be afraid," she whispered to the girl. "We won't hurt you."

The girl's eyes widened for an instant, before she darted out of sight. On a hunch, Eva looked up and caught a glimpse of the girl climbing rapidly up one of the trees.

"Come back," Eva called.

"You found a friend?" Barny gazed up at the trees. The girl had vanished.

"I guess not," Eva said.

"Maybe she didn't understand English."

"Maybe she did," said Agnes.

Eva considered this. A wild child would have no reason to trust them, and every reason not to. She looked around at the watery surroundings and wondered how far they would have to go to find fresh water.

"I think we should head back. We're too far from the ship already," Karin said.

Eva didn't want to argue, but she wasn't ready to give up yet. "Couldn't we just go a little farther? Maybe there's a river feeding into this."

Barny looked at the other sailors. They shrugged. Karin said, "There's still one inch of my skin that doesn't have a mosquito bite."

"Okay. We go a little longer," said Barny.

Minutes later Eva was wiping the sweat off the back of her neck when a sudden downpour drenched her to the skin. Startled, she looked up at the blue sky.

"Somebody up there likes you," Barny said.

Licking her lips, Eva grinned. "It's not salty."

Barny squinted up at the tree. "We don't have time for games. How are you at climbing trees?"

Eva looked at the cypress; its trunk was smooth and limbless, and too big to get her arms around it. "I don't know. Never climbed one that big," she said.

"Then I guess we have to coax her down," said Barny. "Any ideas?"

They were silent in thought until Agnes lifted her face to the treetops and began to sing.

The melody floated through the hot, still air like a cooling zephyr. Eva got chills listening to the words of home far away. The tension in her shoulders loosened as Agnes's lilting voice opened a channel to memories of happier times.

When Agnes came to the end of the song they sat still and waited. For a minute nothing happened, and Barny whispered, "Well, it was nice idea."

A shower of petals fell from above. Not a lot, but enough to make them all look up to see the child holding a branch of some flowering shrub and grinning down on them.

"Hello," Eva said.

The child stopped smiling, but continued to stare at them, subjecting each of them to her piercing gaze.

"Do you know where we can find fresh water?" Barny asked.

The child nodded.

"Would you show us the way?" Barny asked.

The child studied them for another minute before nodding. Then she disappeared behind some leaves. A moment later from a different tree she called, "This way."

They followed her deeper into the swamp. The ground became more solid as they went along. Eva wondered how they would ever find their way back to the ship, but she kept the thought to herself.

At last they came out into a clearing from which a narrow path led into a field of tall grass. The girl appeared from out of the bushes and ran on ahead of them. They trotted after her.

They entered a forest of scrubby pines and live oaks filled with birdsong, and another sound that Eva recognized at once.

"There's a stream," she said, scampering ahead of the others. When she reached the small, clear brook, the girl was kneeling on the opposite bank. She looked at Eva and reached into the stream, cupped her hand and brought it to her lips.

"It's safe to drink?" Eva asked.

The girl swallowed and nodded to Eva.

The others arrived and tested the waters as well. They sat down beside the stream. The girl sat on the other side, watching them.

"Well," said Barny, "I don't know how much good this is going to do us. It'd be a hell of a job to schlepp anything back to the ship from here."

"What choice do we have?" asked Karin.

"None at the moment. Unless our little friend here has any ideas," said Barny, gazing steadily at the wild child, who appeared to be following their conversation.

The girl shook her head slowly.

"Where does this stream go?" Eva asked.

"Turtle Lake," the child said.

"If there's a lake, it's farther away from the shore," said Barny.

"But maybe there's a path or a road or something," said Eva.

"We don't have a cart." Barny shook her head. "Nope. Sorry kid, thanks for the tour but I think we'd best go back to the ship. Fill up your gallon jugs. We can at least carry those back."

Eva glanced at the child. "What about her?"

Barny gave Eva a look. "What about her?"

"Are we going to take her with us? We can't just leave her here alone."

"How do you know she's alone? She might have a whole tribe back at the lake, or wherever she lives," Barny said, lowering a gallon jug into the stream.

"Yeah, but..." Eva noticed the child was watching them intently. "What if she's alone?"

Barny turned on Eva impatiently. "Listen, you don't know anything about this kid. Maybe she's alone, maybe she's not. It's none of our business either way. If she wants to come with us..." she glanced over at the child, whose pale blue eyes were locked on them. Barny sighed heavily.

"What do you think, Agnes? Do we take another kid on board?"

"Why don't we ask her?" Agnes said, smiling at the child. "Would you like to come with us?"

The girl's eyes grew wider. She nodded slowly.

"Won't your momma miss you?" Agnes asked.

The girl shook her head slowly, her smile gone. "My momma died."

"What about your daddy?"

"Never had daddy. Only momma." She took hold of a small locket hanging round her neck and opened it so that Agnes could see the tiny photo inside.

"Is that your momma?"

The girl nodded and gazed steadily at Agnes, who smiled again and said, "Well, that's settled then. Come on. You can help us find our way back to our boat."

The child jumped across the brook and took hold of Agnes's hand.

Barny shook her head. "Fine. Another mouth to feed. You can explain her to the captain."

Eva knelt to bring her face close to the girl's and whispered, "Hi. My name's Eva, what's yours?"

"Sadie."

CHAPTER 19

Eva shaded her eyes with her hand and squinted up at the crow's nest. Nimbly clambering up the mast, faster than any of the crew, Sadie appeared hardly larger than the ship's cat. The tiny girl had the natural balance and sure grip of a circus monkey, with the mischief to match.

In the weeks since they had introduced her to the captain and the rest of the crew, the sailors had gone from tolerating Sadie's presence to seeking her out. Her quick smile and shy giggle helped lift the cloud of brooding uncertainty that had been hovering over the ship since the rains stopped. They still hadn't found a place to land.

Shortly after they had returned to the ship the captain had announced a change of course.

"This is no time of year to be heading north," she said. "I won't risk this ship in the winter storm season. I've had enough of rain. We're heading for Mexico. If it's still there, we can pass the time until the winds change."

"What if they don't change?" Barny asked.

The captain glanced out at the calm sea. "If the Mother has changed the winds... We'll come up with another plan. But until we know different, we're going to sail the way we always have, and hope the winds haven't turned against us."

"What if Mexico's under water too?"

The captain looked to see who'd said this. Agnes lifted her chin and caught the captain's eye. The captain frowned slightly and raised an eyebrow. "Well, Agnes, we can stand here and play 'what if' all day, but that won't get us anywhere. We're just going to keep looking until we find someplace. Unless you have a better idea."

"Nope. Just sayin' out loud what everybody's thinkin'."

The crew murmured among themselves and went back to their chores. Eva returned to the galley to clean fish. Since they had run out of chickens the menu had become monotonously fishy.

Sadie was too small to be much help in the weightier work of sailing, but she made herself useful in small ways, mending nets, sweeping the galley, braiding hair. Her touch was light, and she never said no when anyone asked her to help out. She especially took a shine to Agnes, and always found a spot near the older woman in the evenings, when there was a chance of a song or two.

One night when a half moon was glinting on the sea and the air was soft and quiet, Eva noticed Sadie standing alone at the railing. In one hand the little girl was clutching the tiny locket she wore around her neck. Her other hand was curled into a fist from which she poked out her fingers one by one.

Eva watched her curiously. Catching sight of Agnes, Eva asked, "Why does she do that?"

Agnes looked up. "What do you mean?"

"She stands there and does that thing with her fingers, most every night."

Agnes shrugged. "Why don't you ask her?"

"She doesn't talk."

"She is a quiet one."

"What do you think she's doing when she does that?"

Agnes shrugged again. "If I had to guess, I'd say she was counting something."

"Like the stars, you mean?"

"Maybe. Maybe she counts her blessings. My mother used to do that."

"That kid doesn't have any blessings to count."

Agnes shook her head. "That's where you're wrong. We've all got blessings. Some more than others maybe. But that little girl strikes me as someone who knows what it means to have troubles."

"That's my point. Troubles, yeah. I bet she's got a handful of them."

"And yet she seems happy."

Eva inclined her head. "Maybe she's too dumb to know how unlucky she is."

Agnes gave her a look. "Maybe you're the one who's dumb, not knowing how lucky you are."

"You don't know me."

"So tell me about yourself. What makes you so angry all the time?"

"I'm not angry all the time." Eva scowled as she said it, feeling the burn of resentment glowing in her chest.

"Are you sure?" Agnes asked.

"Just never mind me, okay? I'm fine. I'm happy. Sadie's happy. We're all stuck on this boat forever, it's all good."

"Ease up, child. Things could be a lot worse." Agnes got up and stretched her arms.

"I never said they couldn't. I'm just saying, they could be better."

"Things can always be better, or worse. The trick is to make the most of each moment."

"It's not so easy...when you lose some things."

"You've lost things?"

"Everybody has." Eva lifted her chin as she said this.

"That's true," Agnes agreed. "Some people have lost more than they can count."

"What if you've got nothing left?" Eva asked.

"Everybody's got something," Agnes said. "Even if they lose it. They still had it once. If you had something once, that's something to be thankful for."

"That's crazy. You mean if you had... Let's say you had a castle, and a prince, and a lot of money. And then you lost all those things. You think you still should be thankful for them?"

"Yes. Because some people never have any of those things, not even for one minute. And if you had them, even for one minute, that's something you would never forget, and you can be thankful for that."

Eva shook her head. "Not me. I'd be mad. And I wouldn't be thankful, because I would always remember what I lost."

"But don't you see? You can't lose what you never had. If you had it once, you always have it. Inside of you. That's what my mother told me. Before she was killed."

"I'm sorry," Eva said.

"You don't have to be sorry. She loved me so much, I still feel it. And my father loved me too."

Eva turned to stare at Sadie, who had crept up beside them while they were talking. When Eva looked back at Agnes, the older woman was watching Sadie with a knowing smile.

"Sadie's a very lucky girl," she said.

"What makes you say that?" Eva asked.

Agnes turned to Eva and said, "This child has been loved, and she knows it. You can see it in her eyes, in her smile. That's not something everybody gets to have. The knowledge, the true, deep knowledge that you are worthy of love is something that gives you power no one can take from you." She looked at Sadie, who was smiling at her. "Ain't that right, Sadie girl?"

Sadie nodded, her eyes shining brightly in the darkness.

Eva frowned and turned away.

***

The ship continued on a southwestern course. The sun grew stronger; the days grew longer. The fishing was good. They didn't go hungry.

The crew were in good spirits. Somehow Sadie's presence had been accepted in a different spirit than Eva's. No one ever whispered that the cheerful sprite carried bad luck. Instead, the crew fell into the habit of citing Sadie's cryptic remarks. On the rare occasions when Sadie misplaced a foot as she clambered to the crow's nest, she would shake her head and say, "I got jelly toes today." She had her own way of describing certain kinds of clouds. Sailors as a rule parse cloud formations with colorful flair, but Sadie's slang quickly found favor after she was heard to pronounce a particular formation as turtle poop, and another as snake skin.

One morning in late January the Sierra Madres appeared on the horizon. A cheer went up from the crew. The captain peered unsmiling into a telescope as the ship drew closer to the land.

"Don't see any beaches. No sand. No port town." She turned to the sailors watching her. "Looks like we'll have to hunt around for a safe place to come ashore."

Barny and Karin smiled at each other and stepped forward. The captain rolled her eyes.

"If I send you two again I want it understood you're not to bring back any more pets. Do I make myself clear?"

"Aye, aye, Captain," said Barny. Karin poked her with an elbow. Barny shifted her weight and added, "But, uh, if we do find someone of particular interest?"

The captain heaved a loud sigh. "Come on, Barny. Use your best judgment. I'm fond of our little monkey, but I'm not running a circus. Got it?"

"Aye, aye," said Barny and Karin in unison.

The captain was turning back to look into her telescope when she felt a tug on her jacket. She shook her head as soon as she saw the look in Eva's eyes. "Not a chance, kid. You and Agnes are staying here. You brought back a souvenir last time I let you off the ship. Now you can keep the baby happy. And she's not leaving the ship until we know exactly what we're dealing with."

She turned back to stare into the dark purple folds of the mountains, looming higher and closer with every minute. "If there are people in those mountains, they could be hostile. Or worse."

"What's worse than hostile?" Eva asked.

The captain didn't answer.

Eva walked back to the other side of the ship where Sadie waited beside Agnes.

"We no go?" the little girl asked, looking up at Eva's unsmiling face.

"We no go," Eva responded, meeting Agnes's calm gaze.

"Oh, we don't mind about that, Sadie girl," Agnes said. "We'll be climbing those mountains soon enough, I reckon."

"Me reckon too," Sadie nodded.

Barny and Karin set off within an hour in a pair of row boats with six sailors, two of whom spoke Spanish. They were determined to return with provisions of one sort or another.

The boats began scraping over limbs and branches when they were roughly fifty feet from the new shoreline. Waves foamed over a scraggly rim of sodden branches where oak trees thrust out of the soil. The sailors got out and pulled the boats through the thick tangle underwater to a spot where they could tie up to tree trunks at the edge of a pathless forest.

The hike through woods was slow going, hot and damp. Birds whistled and squawked high above in the fluttering canopy.

After half an hour they came upon a path of dry, beaten dirt. The air was dryer too. Barny said they must be climbing higher. They could feel it in their legs, though it wasn't as perceptible in the dense forest. When they stopped at a fresh stream to fill their canteens, Karin lifted her head and sniffed the air.

"Do you smell that?" she asked.

Barny inhaled deeply. "Smoke."

"Wood smoke. Somebody's cooking," said Karin.

Soon the path led them into a clearing with a dozen huts nestled in the shade around a wide open circle where several women were tending a fire. Children and chickens roamed freely in the sunlight. All the women stopped and stared as the crew stepped into view.

"Hello," said Barny, lifting her open hand in a gesture she hoped would be interpreted as friendly.

The village women stared at them blankly. The children stopped playing and watched them silently.

"Hi," said Karin, with a big smile. "We come in peace. We're looking for food." She motioned as if she were eating, guessing that perhaps these villagers wouldn't understand English. She turned to Inez, one of the Spanish speaking crew members. "See if they understand you."

Inez stepped forward and spoke for a few minutes. The villagers' faces relaxed, and they stared at the sailors with shy smiles. The children ran forward as a pack and then regrouped in front of the sailors. One of the village women came over and began a rapid exchange with Inez.

After a few minutes Inez turned to Barny and said, "The men are out hunting. This woman thinks they would be happy to take us hunting with them tomorrow. She invites us to wait until they get back, and then we can plan what to do tomorrow. They also have some grain they can trade for cloth or other things. She says we can stay here tonight, or go back to the ship and get what we need and stay as long as we need to." Inez shared a smile with the woman before adding, "She was surprised that we're all women. She's not sure what their husbands will think, but she thinks it will be okay."

The crew settled in under a spreading oak to await the return of the men. The village women provided them with a luncheon of soft tortillas and vegetables. The children hung around and stared at them patiently.

"I guess there's not a lot going on around here," said Barny, as she leaned back against a tree.

Inez, who had been chatting with the women who brought the food, said, "Clara says things used to be very hard for them. Before the Greening. The drug business brought in a lot of violence."

"Way out here?" asked Karin.

"Especially out here. Easy access to the ocean, too remote for the Feds. That all ended when the planes stopped flying. She says things have been good lately. She said they used to see dragons, but none have bothered them. She says their village is protected by Golden Eagles."

"I've heard of that," said Barny. "A dealer I knew back in the day once told me that he wasn't scared of the Feds, but the eagles were like monsters. He said the mountain people hold them sacred."

"Ah," said Karin. "That would explain the carvings."

"Carvings?"

"Look at the huts. Over almost every door, or beside it, they've got carved eagle wings. At least one of them has the full eagle," said Karin.

"Whatever gets you through the night," said Barny.

***

When the village men returned, they readily agreed to take the sailors with them on the following day's hunt. They invited the crew to stay for the evening meal, but Barny explained that they had to get back and report to their captain.

The hike back to the boats seemed shorter. And when they arrived back at the ship the captain was so cheered by their good news she declared that a larger group would accompany them back to the village the next day, to carry articles for trading and to enjoy the feel of solid ground under their feet for a few hours.

As it turned out, a few hours stretched into a few weeks. The first day of hunting together was so successful that they had more than enough to carry back to the ship, and the villagers insisted they celebrate together. That night the crew enjoyed a feast washed down by the local brew. There was music and dancing afterward. The men played guitars and other stringed instruments Eva didn't recognize. Several of the men sang, and a few of the women. Eva kept an eye on Sadie during the festivities, noticing how easily the child fit in with the villagers, even though, as far as Eva knew, she didn't speak any Spanish. Maybe being young was enough of a passport, Eva mused.

The music rang through the trees with an intoxicating tempo, and at one point Eva's feet started tapping in spite of her inclination to hang back in the shadows. Suddenly Sadie appeared at her side with an outstretched hand.

"Dance," Sadie commanded in her squeaky voice.

Eva hesitated for only a second before the music pulled her to the circle, where she and Sadie spun and twirled and stamped their feet, laughing as if the world were new again. Stars sparkled overhead and the scent of flowers and wood smoke mingled sweetly in the air.

Later Eva lay down to sleep in one of the two huts set aside for the sailors, her heart still skipping to the the beat of the music, but as her pulse gradually slowed she felt a stinging premonition. In the months she'd been on the ship she'd had a lot of time to reflect on the way the tide of fortune flows back and forth. Nothing this good could last long.

***

For a while, however, the sailors enjoyed a respite from the boredom of an all-fish all-the-time diet. They began to feel almost at home in the company of a cheerful people living in harmony with the serene beauty around them.

The days were filled with simple chores, hunting, cooking and weaving. The evenings ended with a meal around the fire, followed by music and stories.

At one of these gatherings Barny asked Ernesto, the most respected village storyteller, why the villagers had so many images of eagles on their huts.

Ernesto leaned back and turned his face to the stars. The villagers hushed expectantly. In the circle of quiet the hiss and crackle of the fire caught the darkness in a flickering net and drew the villagers closer, and Ernesto began.

When the world was new, in the First Days, the People and the Animals understood one another. The Coyotes spoke to the People. The Mountain Lions taught the People how to hunt.

And the great Thunderbirds kept watch over the village and warned them of storms and enemies.

The People were happy because they lived in a golden age of peace and harmony. Everyone had plenty to eat, and warm fur to wear in the cold months. The Animals and the People treated each other with respect, taking only what they needed to survive.

But after a time strangers from across the Great Water came to this land. They didn't follow the way of the People. They didn't understand the Animals and the Birds. They had weapons of metal and fire, and they killed more than they could eat and left it to spoil. They killed for no reason.

One day a hunter from across the Great Water saw a pair of Thunderbirds flying high above the mountains. The hunter had never seen a creature so magnificent. He followed them for days, climbing higher and higher until he saw the nest they had built at the top of a mighty pine tree. The hunter watched as the birds brought food to feed their children. But the hunter didn't care about the Thunderbirds' children. He wanted their feathers for himself.

So he climbed closer and closer, staying hidden in the forest so the birds would not see him. He waited until the father Thunderbird had flown away to get food. Then he climbed even higher and waited until he could see the mother waiting at the edge of the nest, guarding her children.

The hunter aimed his gun and fired, striking the mother Thunderbird in the heart. She fell from the nest, crashing down through the trees until she landed lifeless on the forest floor.

The hunter quickly climbed down to gather his prize, but the mother Thunderbird was so huge he couldn't carry her. He tried to drag her body, but he was soon worn out and lay down to rest.

The father Thunderbird, meanwhile, had returned to the nest and learned from his children what had happened. In a fury he flew out and searched the forest until he found the sleeping hunter. He snatched the murderer in his talons and carried him high over the jagged rocks. The hunter was awakened by this and screamed and pleaded for mercy, but the Thunderbird was too angry. After he dropped the hunter to his death, Thunderbird returned and carried the body of his mate to a cave high up on the cold mountain, where no human could scavenge her beautiful feathers.

The Thunderbird was so filled with rage and grief that he screeched and clawed at the rocks. Wondering how he could take care of his children alone, he flew above the village of the People and saw a beautiful young girl cradling an infant in her arms. She was too young to be a mother, but she was charged with caring for the village children while their parents worked. This gave Thunderbird an idea.

He flew down and spoke to the village elder and explained how his mate had been murdered, and how he needed someone to help him raise his children.

The people of the village listened to him politely, but they were reluctant to send one of their own daughters to help him.

They asked him why he didn't steal a woman from the other humans, since they were the ones who took his wife. But Thunderbird said he wouldn't trust those humans to care for his children. That is why he came to the People. And then they understood. So they had a meeting and decided to ask for a volunteer.

At first no one stepped forward. But then the chief's son spoke and reminded them how the Thunderbirds had always looked after the People and protected them from their enemies. "Surely we owe Thunderbird this small favor," he said.

Now the young girl who had been looking after the village children was known as Sowetta. She was a quiet maid whose parents had died when she was very young and she had no one to stand up for her. She had always loved the chief's son, even though he had never noticed her. So she considered what he had said, and decided that maybe if she did this thing for the Thunderbird, the chief's son would think well of her.

So she volunteered. And the whole village was happy because no one else had to give up a daughter. No one really believed that the girl would be returned to the village once the baby Thunderbirds were grown. They imagined she would be eaten.

But Sowetta wasn't afraid. She walked up to the Thunderbird and said, "I will go with you." The Thunderbird inclined his giant head and told her to climb on his back. She did, and held on to his feathers. Soon they were flying high above the village. Once they arrived at the nest Sowetta met the baby Thunderbirds. There were four of them, all just beginning to get feathers. At first they weren't sure whether she was food or not, but their father quickly explained that she was there to take care of them. And so it was.

The Thunderbird had to work even harder to feed the children now, and he also had to bring food for Sowetta. She wasn't used to raw meat, but she made the best of it, and always waited until the children finished their food before she ate a bite.

At night she curled up under the Thunderbird's feathers and slept comfortably in the nest as it swayed gently high above the world.

Days went by, and weeks, and Sowetta came to love the faithful Thunderbird for his selfless nobility and gentle way with her. For his part, the Thunderbird was grateful for Sowetta's patience and cheerful strength. She never complained. She always welcomed him back to the nest with a smile and sometimes she sang sweet songs to the children, a thing the mother Thunderbird hadn't been able to do.

Gradually, Sowetta fell in love with the Thunderbird. She didn't know what could come of this, so she tried not to let him see. But after several months, when it would soon be time for the young Thunderbirds to leave the nest, she knew she had to say something. So one night, as they lay cradled together, she said, "Lord Thunderbird, you are the finest creature I have ever known. If only I could be your wife, I would be the happiest of women."

Thunderbird sighed and caressed her small head with one feather. "I care for you also," he said. "But I cannot mate with someone who cannot fly. To be a Thunderbird is to fly."

"How can I possibly fly?" Sowetta cried. "Couldn't we go on like this, as we have been?"

"No my dear. After the children leave, you must return to your People, and I must search for a new mate."

"But I'm your mate!" she lamented.

"I'm sorry. That can never be unless you die and are reborn as a Thunderbird," he said.

That night while Thunderbird slept beside her, Sowetta thought and thought about her life, and her future. She knew if she went back to her village no man would ever want the girl who had slept with the Thunderbird. And she had no desire for anyone else.

The next day the Thunderbird flew off to get food as usual. The children, by now so large they nearly crowded her out of the nest, squawked and hopped eagerly awaiting his return. Sowetta hugged them each in turn and then climbed to stand on the edge of the nest, overlooking the canyon far below.

She held her arms out wide as if to embrace the sky. "Tell your father to look for me," she said, and leapt to her death.

When Thunderbird returned and learned what had happened he was stunned with grief. He flew off to search for her. Her body was never found. Thunderbird has been searching for her ever since.

Eva lay awake for hours that night, envying the strength of the villagers' beliefs, and the comfort their shared myths gave them. She thought about her own upbringing, and how she had learned to doubt everything and trust no one. Not even her own mother.

She sighed and listened to the night birds calling in the darkness. Everything in the mountain jungle seemed to have a purpose. Yet when Eva tried to weigh out her own conflicting desires, they vanished as if made of smoke. She no longer felt any ambition to regain her magical power and rule her own territory. The hollowness suddenly yawned before her mind like a barren canyon. What good would it do to get it all back, even if she could? A vision of Clayton suddenly rose before her mind's eye, and she heard his voice, challenging her to do something worthwhile with her powers. She winced as she recalled how she had scoffed at his idealism.

She rolled over on the hard ground and pulled her blanket closer.

***

Eva began trying to make herself useful to the villagers. She volunteered to carry water, to grind corn, to feed the elders who had lost their ability to care for themselves. She remembered being forced to go with Josh to visit his mother in the nursing home. Eva had hated every minute of those trips—the smells, the vacant looks on the faces of the residents. They seemed so lost and frightened. Eva couldn't stand to be around them, and she didn't understand why Josh bothered to visit his withered old mother.

Yet as she wiped the mouth of one of the village great-grandmothers, a wisp of a woman whose toothless smile still shone even though she could no longer walk, Eva sensed that the old woman was at peace with life itself.

She wished she could talk to the woman and learn what life had taught her. But Eva's Spanish was primitive, and she didn't know how to begin.

When she had nothing to do, which was often, she watched the village children, whose games swirled around the open space like leaves tossed in the wind. They sang songs and chased one another; they tossed dried gourds and jumped rope. In their company Sadie had blossomed. Eva even saw her taking part in one of the most popular games, playing the golden eagle, flapping arms like wings and chasing each other.

Eva tried to remember a time from her own childhood when she had felt so carefree, but her only memories were of carefully managed parties where the hovering adults suppressed the noise level, and the children were kept to tight schedules. Eva never fit in, in part because her mother was rarely around. Josh had tried to fill the gap, but he wasn't comfortable around all the mothers, some of whom paid more attention to him than to their children.

A loud shriek broke through Eva's daydreaming, and she startled into alertness, looking for Sadie. The children were clustered together at the edge of the forest. One of the little boys had captured a small snake and was brandishing it above his head. Eva looked for Sadie in the group and saw her staring coolly at the boy. She said something Eva couldn't hear, and the boy turned on her, shaking the snake in her face. Sadie waggled her head and said something else that drew laughter from the other children. The boy glared at them for half a second, then he turned back to Sadie and threw the snake at her. She took one small step to the side to allow the snake to sail by her, then stood shaking her head at the boy.

For a moment Eva worried that the embarrassed boy might try to hurt Sadie, but the little girl tipped her head to one side and smiled at the boy, and said something that seemed to appease him. One of the girls grabbed Sadie's hand and they went skipping back across the circle.

Eva watched the other children follow in the zigzagging manner of a flock of birds. She wished she knew what Sadie had said to the boy.

***

The weeks went by and the days grew hotter. The sailors began to grow restless. When they announced their decision to leave, the villagers insisted on one final farewell celebration. As the day neared, Eva noticed that Sadie, usually so sunny and upbeat, had lost her sparkle.

Watching Sadie playing in the dirt with the village children, Eva was distracted for a moment by a raptor riding the thermals high above. When she looked back at the children, for a moment she couldn't see Sadie, until she realized that Sadie was right in plain sight, so much a part of the group that she no longer stuck out as a stranger. Eva was unnerved as an unwelcome thought entered her mind.

Later, when Eva lay down on her blanket next to Sadie, she saw the little girl's eyes shining in the darkness, staring at her.

"What is it, Sadie?"

"Sadie want to stay."

Eva flinched at the words, though she had almost expected them. "Stay where?"

"Here. Not go on boat. This my home now."

Eva felt the truth of it, even as she tried to think of a reason Sadie should come with her. "Are you sure that's what you want? I wish you would stay with me."

Sadie rolled closer and put her small hand on Eva's cheek. "Sadie never forget," she said.

Eva blinked hard to squelch the tears that stung behind her eyes. "If you ever need me, I'll come to you," she said, taking hold of Sadie's hand.

Sadie smiled then.

On the night before the ship was to depart, the villagers brought gifts for the crew. Sadie was already wearing hers, a fur-lined goat leather vest from the family she would be staying with when the crew left.

Eva sat next to Agnes listening to the sad sweet music at the last campfire.

"Where are we going when we leave?" Eva asked.

Agnes shrugged. "Where is there to go? I suppose we'll head north, northeast. Some of the girls had families up around Boston way. Might be they had to move to higher ground. Only one way to find out."

"Hasn't JayPeg heard how things are by now?"

"Too many rumors. Hard to know where the truth lies." Agnes turned away from the firelight and measured Eva with a look. "How about you? Anyone back on land you'd like to check up on?"

Eva's brow furrowed. She'd been thinking a lot about her mother and Josh. And Clayton. She didn't want to talk about it, but in the long nights she had been struggling with unfamiliar feelings of guilt and anxiety. The notion that she may have been unfair to her mother had been sneaking into her mind and making faces at her. Eva had been so sure of herself that it came as an unpleasant discovery to realize that she missed her mother. And Clayton. And even Josh. She tried not to think about Mudley. Surely a dog wouldn't even notice how long she'd been gone. But Eva couldn't deny that she worried that her faithful dog might be feeling abandoned.

She replied, "Yeah. There're a few people I'd like to see."

"Well, then. Cheer up. We're going home tomorrow."

Eva pursed her lips together, stumbling on the concept of "home." She wasn't sure where it was anymore.

***

In the morning the sun shone with a clarity that made every wet leaf gleam like an emerald. Eva shielded her eyes as she gazed up to the mountain tops, where several eagles were circling.

The villagers had all come out to see the sailors off. The children clustered around Sadie, alternately hugging and chasing her. Eva was turning to take a final look at the village circle, wondering if she would ever really return, when a sudden uproar rose from the children. They had put some distance between themselves and the adults, but greater still was the distance between Sadie and the other children.

She was skipping beyond their reach, teasing them with a little song. The looks of horror on their faces must have struck her as odd, for she turned to look behind her just as an enormous eagle dropped from the sky and snatched her in its talons.

The children shrieked as the eagle hurtled back into the clouds, while the adults raced to the spot where Sadie had stood only seconds before. Breathless with shock, Eva stared at the speck vanishing in the clear blue sky.

A hush fell over the children as they turned their wide eyes on Eva. She asked Ernesto, "How far is it to the eagle's nest?"

Sylvia translated the question to Ernesto. He shook his head and replied briefly.

"He says no one can reach that eagle's nest. He says that was no ordinary eagle. It was too big." Sylvia frowned before she continued. "He says he has never seen a thunderbird before."

"That was a thunderbird? But I thought they were just legends."

Sylvia exchanged more words with the old man. Then she said, "He says some people say thunderbirds still exist in the highest mountains. He says if it was a thunderbird that took Sadie...she will never be returned."

"But we're going to try to rescue her, aren't we?" Eva asked, looking at the captain.

The captain shook her head. "I'm sorry, kid. There's nothing we can do. Even if we could find the nest, even if we managed to reach it, she wouldn't be... She wouldn't be alive by the time we got there."

"You don't know that!" Eva said.

The captain took a long breath and said quietly, "Everyone knows that. You know it." She stepped closer and tried to put an arm around Eva's shoulders. Eva shook it off angrily. "Listen, kid. It's a terrible thing. And we're all sorry it happened. But it's over now." The captain pursed her lips for a second before continuing. "At least she was happy these last few weeks. If it wasn't for you, she wouldn't have had that."

"If it wasn't for me she would still be back in the swamp in Carolina. Alive."

Agnes edged closer and said, "Eva, it's not your fault. Sadie had her own destiny. You have yours. That's the way life is."

"Don't talk about her as if she's already dead. She could be alive right now. Fighting to escape, hurt and scared and—" Eva crumpled to the ground, unable to hold back her tears.

After more discussion the village elders told the captain that they would send their best hunters to find the bird's nest and rescue Sadie if she was still alive. Eva asked to go along, but the elders insisted the hunters would have a better chance of success on their own.

Eva couldn't argue in a language she didn't speak.

The trip back to the ship, anticipated with enthusiasm a few hours earlier, took place in silence. The heavy, humid air weighed them down even more as the sun rose higher and the temperature climbed. By the time they finished loading their fresh supplies onboard the tide had shifted.

Eva stood at the rail staring back at the mountains, her face a mask of misery.

JayPeg came up and leaned on the rail beside her. Eva shot a threatening look at her. JayPeg remained silent beside her for the better part of an hour while the ship slowly moved away from the shore. As she was turning to leave, Eva grabbed her forearm and looked into her eyes. "Do you think she could be alive?" she asked.

JayPeg tilted her head to one side and said, "Stranger things have happened. She was... *is* a tough little kid. If anyone could, she would."

Eva closed her eyes and took a deep shuddering breath, before she replied.

"Thanks. I just... you know..."

"Yeah. I know.

***

Her ribs ached. Her hands were scratched and bleeding. It was cold this high up. She bent her head to feel the fur against her cheek. The vest was gashed, but it had saved her life, cushioning her against the blunt force of the eagle's talons.She had nearly swooned from the pain and the shock at first, but the cold air rushing against her and the thrill of soaring thousands of feet above the ground had kept her alert. She knew she wouldn't have much time once the eagle let go. Her only thought was to dive off the edge of wherever it landed, and hope there would be something to cling to.

In the split second after the eagle released its grip on her, she scrambled out from under it and scrabbled down the side of the nest. The nest was old and densely packed with thick branches, secured in the junction of two large limbs of the pine. She found a small gap between the bottom of the nest and the limb below it and wedged herself into it.

Now, still and silent, she waited for the eagle to leave. She hoped it wasn't waiting for its mate to return. She was hungry and cold. But she wasn't tired yet. She knew she was a hundred feet off the ground—a hard climb in the best of circumstances, and she had an idea that would make the climb even harder. But she hadn't come this far to return empty-handed.

Sadie grinned at the cloudless blue sky and settled down to outwait the giant bird.

PART THREE

In the shadowy folds of the Blue Ridge ancient forces were stirring, shaken from centuries of slumber by the magic trickling down between layers of rock and mineral. Fingerlings of life crept and clawed toward the surface, gaining speed as they neared the soft, penetrable skin of earth. When they burst into the light they grew with rapacious and reckless abandon, snarling, twining, thorny spikes piercing virgin bark, climbing higher, wider.

In the quiet foothills, few men attempted to wrest a living from this land. The rocks and trees closed ranks in mockery of man's limited reach. Those stubborn souls who refused to leave came to resemble the gnarled woods. They avoided other humans, and put what faith they had in the trees themselves.

As time passed, wildness regained what had been lost in the age of machines and destruction. And as the magic spread, wildness grew wilder than ever.

CHAPTER 20

The scent of lilacs crept into Shiloh's dream. A memory of her mother's garden bloomed in her sleep and she sat up quickly, blinking in momentary confusion at the soft spring sunlight filtering in from the window.

Josh stood by the bed, backlit by the morning light, a bouquet of lilac in his hand. "Good morning. I didn't mean to startle you. Mrs. Fitzsimmon down the street gave me these when I went out to get the eggs."

The new normal settled on Shiloh's consciousness, shredding the dream-conjured memories of more innocent times. "Oh," she said. "That was nice of her."

Josh sat down beside her. "You okay?" he asked.

She took a deep breath. "Yeah. Sure." She closed her eyes briefly. "I'm okay."

"I thought maybe instead of having breakfast here we could go out for a picnic brunch down in the park. It's a nice morning."

Shiloh got out of bed and started to pull clothes out of drawers. Simple actions to blunt the memories of other Easters. Baskets, chocolates, bunny toys. Eva.

"I heard they're going to have the Egg Roll at the White House this year," Josh said.

"Really? That'd be the first time since..."

"Yeah."

"I'm surprised they're going to waste the eggs," she said.

"They're not."

She raised an eyebrow.

"They got a bunch of smooth rocks and painted them and they're calling it the Easter Egg Rock 'n' Roll. They're going to have bands and stuff."

Shiloh grinned and shook her head. "I guess the parents will like that."

"And the little kids won't know the difference."

Shiloh stopped smiling. "Yeah. Just like they'll never know what a real tiger looks like."

"Aren't there still a few left in zoos?"

"Last time I checked there was one in Germany and one in Philadelphia. But I don't think there's a breeding pair left."

Josh came closer and wrapped an arm around her shoulders. "It's too bad about the tigers. But... life goes on. And... you know... we could... now that you don't have to go save the world anymore..."

She pulled away and looked into his eyes. "What are you suggesting?"

"Why shouldn't we? I love you. You love me. And the world needs more children. We've lost so much in the last ten years. And our child would be—"

"Are you crazy? I don't want to bring another child into this messed up world. And even if I did, I don't have the right to ruin another child's life."

"You never ruined anyone's life."

"I was a terrible mother."

"No you weren't."

"Yes I was. I lied to her. I abandoned her. She hates me, and I can't blame her."

"She loves you, and she'll come back. I know she will. She just needs to figure some things out. Once she does, she'll come back."

"Why should she? She certainly doesn't need me. And it's pretty obvious she'll never trust me again." She shook her head. "It's hopeless."

Josh hugged her and said, "Nothing's hopeless. The worst is over. The magic's gone. We have a chance to make a better world. And our child could grow up in it."

"I'm too old. I'm worn out. I wasn't a good mother in my twenties. What makes you think I'd do better in my forties?"

"You were just a kid yourself eighteen years ago. And we'd be together." His dark brown eyes stared deeply into hers, and she could see how much he wanted this. But she wasn't convinced it would be fair to the child.

She took another deep breath and said, "I'll think about it, okay?"

He nodded. "Come on, let's have a picnic. I bought muffins and berries. You're going to love it."

"Will there be coffee?" she asked as they started down the stairs.

"The thermos is full of it," he said.

"You make it too easy for me," she said with a smile.

As they strolled down P Street, Shiloh had to admit she felt more optimistic than she had in a while. The kinder light of spring seemed to lift the mood of the city. Children with baskets and balloons were out in numbers. At the ridge of the park there were dozens of other couples, and a few whole families spread out on the bank above the water. Since the flood, the formerly modest creek for which the park had been named had swelled to grander proportions. The bridges at P and Q Streets that had once arched thirty feet above the water now spanned the distance between the banks a mere ten feet from the water's surface. Where once visitors used to wade among the rocks that jutted out of the creek, they now rowed boats rented from Thompson's, relocated to higher ground. Wading across the creek was a thing of the past.

The shadow of a hovercraft sped across the grass. Shiloh glanced up, squinting into the sun. "I can't get used to how quiet those things are," she said.

"Yeah. Kind of creepy. But they're a big improvement on the old choppers."

Shiloh watched the hovercraft skim above the trees, heading to the White House. "I guess I should be glad. At least they're not spewing oil fumes."

"Big oil's dead. They'll never be able to restore the whole infrastructure. Mag-lev is here to stay," Josh said.

"I hope you're right."

They found a patch of shade in which to spread their blanket and set out their picnic. While they ate, Shiloh's gaze wandered to the woods on the opposite bank. The sunlight shimmering on the creek sent flickering reflections into the trees.

"Boy, the light over there really looks different, doesn't it?" said Josh.

Shiloh stared into the shadows behind the trees.

Josh looked at her. "Are you okay?"

"I don't know." After a few minutes she got up and walked a few feet to the right, staring across the creek the whole time. Then she walked back and peered from the other side of their picnic spot.

"What is it?" Josh asked.

"There's something..." she frowned. "When you look over there, no, there, above that big white rock." She pointed, then looked around cautiously to check that no one was watching her.

"What am I supposed to be seeing?" Josh asked.

"You shouldn't be seeing anything. But...do you?"

Josh shrugged. "I don't know. There's that funny light thing. It's probably just reflecting off the river."

Shiloh pursed her lips. Then she started packing up the picnic.

"What? Are we done already?"

"I need to go look at that thing. Closer. You want to come with?"

He shrugged again. "I guess. What do you think it is?"

Shiloh didn't say anything until they had finished packing up and were walking across the bridge. "You know what I think it is."

"I do?"

"Think about it."

"Um. I'm feeling kind of stupid, but I don't really have any idea, unless... Do you think it's—"

"I think it's a vent. It's a vent I used a lot, back before the Rain. But then you couldn't see it from across the creek. You could hardly see it when you were right up next to it. Now, even you can see it. A hundred yards away."

Josh frowned slightly. "Well, so what? Just because we can see it doesn't mean—"

"I don't know what it means. And neither do you. But something tells me it's not good."

As they drew closer to the wooded spot Shiloh slowed down, then stopped at the edge of the trees.

"I thought you wanted to get a closer look," Josh said.

Shiloh stared at the gauzy slice of air. It was shimmying like a hula dancer and almost as enticing. "This is close enough. There are too many people around. I don't want anyone to see us and get curious. It's so exposed." She looked back at the picnickers across the creek. "If people start going into the vents..."

Josh reached for her hand. "Hey. You can't worry about every little thing that might happen. It's not very likely anyway. It's off the beaten path."

"Maybe. But there are hundreds...maybe thousands of them all over the world. People will get curious and explore them. You know they will." She sighed. "Let's go home. I don't want to draw attention to it by staring at it."

On the walk back Shiloh was quiet, thinking about the last time she'd been through the vent. She was lost in thought when she stumbled on a crooked brick in the sidewalk and clutched Josh's arm for balance. He smiled, and she felt the familiar guilt at how easily she fell into the habit of taking him for granted. She smiled back and said, "What are you so happy about?"

"Oh, I was just thinking I forgot to tell you that your father called."

Shiloh stopped walking. "Why didn't you tell me? Didn't he want to talk to me? When did he call?"

"I didn't talk to him. He left a message while I was out getting the eggs. I guess you didn't hear the phone."

Shiloh started walking faster. "What did he say? I should call him."

"No. It's all right. You don't have to call him. He just called to say he was leaving on a trip. He might come see us."

"What? What kind of a trip? Why?"

Josh shrugged. "It was a short message. He said he wanted to let us know that he was going away for a while and we shouldn't worry. He said he would call again when he can."

A queasy doubt lodged in Shiloh's gut. "That doesn't sound right. Why wouldn't he tell us where he's going?"

"Maybe he didn't want to leave a long message. You know. Some people don't like talking to machines."

Shiloh nodded but her frown remained. "It just doesn't sound right."

"Maybe he's lonely. Maybe he's restless, down there all by himself."

"I wonder if he called Eli. I should call him."

"If your dad didn't call him, you'd only make Eli worry too."

"Right. I guess. Damn. I wish I'd heard the phone. I want to listen to the message."

"Okay. He really didn't say much."

Shiloh shook her head. "So why did he call?" She tried to calm herself, but her father never called just to talk.

***

Brendan hung up the phone and frowned at the counter. *Shouldn't have left a message. Now she'll worry. Can't be helped.* He'd hoped to hear her voice one more time, in case he didn't make it back.

He couldn't explain over the phone anyway. But the dreams were getting stronger. If they were dreams. He wasn't sure anymore. The voices in his head were getting more insistent, interrupting him even in the daytime. Calling for help. Night and day. Of course, it made sense. They had to be calling from all over the world. Some were angry. Some were desolate. They sounded fearful.

Brendan remembered how weak and confused he had felt. Without Shiloh's help he doubted he could have survived. Even with it, there were things he'd never had the heart to tell her. The pain, the despair, the terror. He'd tried to spare her all of that. Her heart was too soft. He didn't want to worry her anymore.

He knew she wouldn't approve of his plan. But he had to go, before the voices drove him insane.

How could he tell her? *Sometimes I wish I were back in the tree.*

CHAPTER 21

Jack stood on the beach watching Magda's dragon approach. Its hot breath caught the evening light, leaving a pink trail in the sky.

The instant her beast touched the sand Magda leapt down and fixed Jack with a scorching glare.

"This had better be good, Jackie Boy," she snarled.

Jack's face registered mild surprise. "Really? That's how you greet me, after I go out of my way to accommodate your absurd demands?"

"As far as I can tell, you haven't given up anything. And what have you done with the girl? I thought we had an agreement. She's off-limits."

Jack held up a hand to refute this charge. "I don't know what you're talking about. If you're referring to little Eva, I certainly haven't had anything to do with her in months. I don't even know where she is."

Magda lowered her chin and leveled a penetrating stare at him. "If you're lying to me..."

Jack snorted. "Please. Why in the Gods' names would I lie to you? You knew I was keeping an eye on Shiloh all those years ago. And I freely admit that I was trying to watch over her daughter until recently, when she dropped out of sight. I thought perhaps you had a hand in it."

The murmur of the waves at the shoreline beside them took on a more melodious tone.

"Oh, damn. Is she here already?" Magda muttered.

Jack smirked. "Now, now, our fair sister wouldn't have called us together if it weren't important. Perhaps she has some insights to share regarding the missing brat."

Magda scowled and watched the sea, where a silvery ship had risen to the surface and now bobbed glistening in the golden light of the sunset. A lean and muscular crew readied a smaller craft, lowering it into the foaming surf. Then a door slid open and from it emerged Cyrene, clad in a glistening opalescent gown. She boarded the shuttle and only then turned her gaze upon the pair waiting on the shore.

Moments later she stepped onto the sand and bowed slightly in their direction. They returned the courtesy, though Jack noticed Magda gritting her teeth.

"Thank you for coming," Cyrene began.

"Did we have a choice?" Magda asked.

Cyrene didn't exactly smile, but she nodded in acknowledgement of Magda's testy mood.

"Dearest Magda, honored Jack, I asked you here today because recent developments on Earth have spread to the very borders of our world. As long as I believed this was harmless, I felt we could ignore the situation. But in the last few months things have become more complicated, and I think the time has come to take action."

"Didn't we already take action? We neutralized the contagion Jack spilled on Earth. I thought the problem was solved." Magda flared her nostrils and folded her arms across her chest. "What's changed?"

Cyrene nodded quietly, her sapphire tiara glinting in the long rays of evening light. "It's true that for a while it appeared that the problem was contained, but it's long been clear that the Deep Magic was more stubborn and stronger than we thought. Our efforts to mitigate the damage through constant vigilance were not enough. Shiloh Carter, with all her skills and magical tools, could not keep up. And the Mother finally lost patience."

"What do you mean?" Jack asked.

Cyrene paused for one moment before she replied. "She sent the Rain."

Jack shot a glance at Magda, whose look of irritation had given way to concern. Magda stared at Cyrene. Seagulls squawked in the air above them. The waves whispered among themselves.

"*The* Rain?" Magda asked.

Cyrene nodded gently.

"Wait," said Jack. "Are we talking the forty-day kind?"

Cyrene shook her head. "The Mother showed mercy this time. The Rain lasted only thirty days."

"When did this happen?" Jack asked.

"It began in the eleventh month of the human calendar," Cyrene said. "It was enough to cleanse the planet. There can never be certainty with magic, as you both well know. But for all intents and purposes, all the magic available to humans, or active on Earth at the time of the Rain, has been washed out, or at least hidden."

"Even if it was..." Jack frowned.

"Even if a human had ingested, inhaled, or been inoculated with magic, it has been washed away." Cyrene watched Jack working through this idea.

After a minute he said, "So that's why I haven't been able to see Eva."

"Precisely," said Cyrene. "You will have noticed that she and Shiloh are no longer visible in the magical spectrum."

"Are they still alive?" Magda asked.

"Yes. Eva..." Cyrene paused, choosing her words with care. "Eva had been abusing her power for some time. The Mother was prepared to sacrifice the child, but I begged Her to give the girl one more chance, and, Gods be good, She consented. She wrapped the girl in Her embrace and cleansed her of the poisonous magical taint. Now Eva is only a young woman like other young women. She's been given a second chance."

"What about Shiloh?" Jack asked. "She never hurt anyone."

"No. Shiloh has been forced to dedicate her life to stopping the spread of magic. Now at last she has a chance to live a life of her own."

"Well, gee. That all sounds swell," Magda scoffed. "But what about us? Is the Mother happy now? Or is She planning to use Her magicide on Theatros too?"

"At this time, I think She is satisfied that balance has been restored between the worlds. That can always change, of course, if some fool acts recklessly." Cyrene glanced at Jack. "As long as we all keep faith with the Mother, She will allow us to go on as we have been for these many centuries."

"Huh," Magda grunted. "I guess it could have been worse."

"It was costly for the humans," Cyrene said. "Millions of lives were lost in the Rain. Cities disappeared. Islands vanished. Coastlines...well, you can imagine. And all of this coming on top of the chaos of the Greening has been hard on the children of Earth. But they are a resilient species. They will recover. And we must leave them in peace to do so."

"So that's what this is about?" Magda huffed.

Cyrene raised her eyebrows. "Yes, Magda. That's what this is about. You and Jack have been known to amuse yourselves at Earth's expense. That must stop. The Mother has spoken."

"Through you," Jack sneered.

"You're free to take the matter up with Her yourself if you like."

Jack rolled his eyes and shook his head. "Why didn't you make Rufio come for this lecture?"

Cyrene smiled gently. "It's well known that Rufio has no interest in Earth or its people."

"Hah. Shows how much you know," Jack muttered.

Magda chuckled. "Oh cheer up, Jack. You know the humans will muck it up soon enough and we'll have new fun with them."

Jack shrugged. "I suppose you're right. I really liked that kid, though. There was something about her."

"Don't despair. We can get you a puppy. Or a baby troll. You'd like that."

"Shut up."

CHAPTER 22

Long before they came in sight of the city skyline, the stench told them they were close. As the ship drew nearer they could see dark smoke rising into the clouds.

"What is that?" Eva asked the captain.

The captain sniffed the air and said, "Burning bodies."

JayPeg came up beside Eva and stared at the once-great city, smoldering in the dusk. Few lights shone from the skyscrapers. Most had become too dangerous to inhabit since the flooded subway tunnels had damaged foundations across the city.

"We shouldn't get any closer," JayPeg said.

"I wasn't planning on it," said the captain. "I just hope none of those scavengers try to take us on."

"They wouldn't do that, would they?" Eva asked.

The captain shrugged. "Desperate people do crazy things." She glanced at Eva. "I wouldn't have brought us this close but we need to find someplace safe to put you ashore. And it's no place near here."

Eva stared at the dark silhouette of the Empire State building. "I guess there's not a lot of food there."

JayPeg said, "From what I hear on the radio, they're working things out. It's the new Venice. No streets, no tunnels. But they're building bridges between upper stories. Still too many bodies floating in the water. The funeral pyres are what you smell. That and the sewage. And...well, you know. People getting killed for safe drinking water."

"Oh my god," Eva breathed. "I just kind of never thought it through. What it would be like."

"Yeah. Nobody did," JayPeg said.

"They'll get through this," the captain said. "New York is unstoppable."

Eva leaned over the rail and threw up. When she was finished, JayPeg handed her a cup of water and said, "Anyone you knew in there?"

"No. But... my mom lived in D.C. I don't know what it's like there."

"They're better off. They're farther inland, and they can still get supplies from growers nearby. It's not like this. New York was an island already, so they got hit pretty bad. And they had a lot more people to start with." She paused. "Not so many now."

Eva was silent, lost in recollections of her mother and Josh. In all the months since she'd been pulled from the sea by the crew of the FaldeRal, she'd barely given a thought to her mother, and how the Rain would have affected her. The chilling realization came to her that she had no idea where her mother had been when the Rain began. She didn't even know if she was dead or alive.

"Are you okay?" JayPeg asked. "Maybe you should lie down. You look like you saw a ghost."

Without a word Eva stumbled to the stairs and went below. She lay for hours on her narrow, hard bed grappling with regrets and memories.

When JayPeg finally came to check on her, Eva was sitting up, dry-eyed, determined to try to make things right if she still could.

"There's food if you're hungry," JayPeg said.

Eva nodded. "Yeah. I better eat. I've got a lot to do."

***

Two days later Eva stepped off the skiff and scrambled up the bank of the Hudson River. She turned to wave to JayPeg.

"Thanks for the lift," she said.

JayPeg was staring at her with an expression Eva couldn't read. JayPeg said something to the sailor at the tiller and stepped out of the boat quickly, closing the distance to Eva.

"Listen," she said quietly, "I know you have people you need to check on here but...I just want you to know that...if things don't work out the way you hope, you could always come back to me. To the ship, I mean."

To her surprise Eva saw a hint of shyness in the older woman's face. "Um, thanks," she said. "I don't know if I'm cut out for the life at sea."

JayPeg reached out and touched her wrist gently. "We wouldn't have to stay on the ship if you didn't want to. I mean. You could be with me. We could make a different life. Together."

Eva stared at her, as understanding dawned. "Oh. I... I'm... I never thought about it."

JayPeg laughed softly. "Really? The whole all-girl-crew thing never gave you any ideas?"

Eva smiled sheepishly. "I guess it never seemed odd to me."

"Exactly. I could tell you were different. I mean... I understand if you don't see me that way. And this is kind of sudden. It's hard to have privacy on a small ship. I didn't want to put you on the spot. But... If you think you could..." She shrugged. "I think we'd be great together."

Eva smiled. "Thanks. I think we might be too." She bit her lip. "But—I have to take care of some things."

"Right. Of course. Just wanted to put that out there for you to have in your back pocket just in case..."

Eva said, "Thanks. I'll think about it."

"Okay. Be careful, kid. Hope I'll see you again." JayPeg turned and started back to the rowboat, but she stopped after a few steps and turned back. She shifted her feet and said, "And take this." She pulled a gold watch from her back pocket and held it out to Eva.

Eva gaped at it. "You don't have to do that."

"It's not mine. Somebody took it off a yacht. You're going to need something to trade for a horse."

Eva took it. She hugged JayPeg and said, "Thanks. I'll pay you back someday."

"You just did," JayPeg said with a grin.

Eva watched as the skiff pulled out into the river, and waved until it was out of sight. Then she stood still, listening to the birds in the trees. She'd never paid much attention to such things before, when she was working to establish herself as the ruler of her little queendom. But now she inhaled the scent of the muddy shore and listened to the rustle of feathers above and thought of Sadie. Her brow pinched together as she tried to push the memory deeper. No time for tears now. She had miles to cover before she got close enough even to see her castle. If it was still there.

On the long trip back from Mexico to the lower New York Bay she had spent hours wondering how the Rain had affected her magic castle. She had tried to brace herself for the possibility that there would be nothing left at all, but she couldn't help hoping that somehow it had survived. Maybe the magic had been strong enough to protect the castle.

And once she reunited with Clayton and Mudley, she would rebuild her forces and set out on a mission to rescue Sadie. It was all so clear to her now.

She traded the watch for a horse at the first town she came to. It was an old horse, not exactly what Eva was hoping for, but the man who sold it to her said she was lucky to get any horse. He frowned at the sight of the watch and muttered, "Nobody wants these things, but if that's all you got..."

Eva thanked him and asked if he had any advice for the route to the Hudson Valley.

The trader squinted at her. "Ain't much up that way anymore. Most folks left years ago. Them as was left lost most of what they had in the Rain. You got people up there?"

"I don't know. I did. I've been away."

"Well, they ain't many roads left going that way. They was some, but since the Rain most of them was lost to thickets."

"There must be ways around them."

The man shook his head slowly. "I don't know of anybody that's got round 'em or past 'em."

"Can't you go through them?"

The man snorted. "I heard some folks took axes to a thicket and tried to cut through it."

"And?"

"They say the thicket yanked the axes out of their hands and knocked 'em off their feet. When they tried to grab the axes, the vines pulled 'em into the thicket and that was the last anyone saw of them."

"The axes or the people?"

"Both. Disappeared. The thicket took 'em inside and they never come out."

"That sounds like magic. I thought all of that got washed away."

The trader shrugged. "Maybe it was. Maybe it wasn't." He gave Eva a calculating look. "Some things don't come out in the wash."

Later, after Eva had secured a few supplies and a saddle, she started north. Clouds flocked the late afternoon sky, glowing in the sunshine. The empty road was narrow, its edges completely transformed with chicory and witchgrass, burdock and milkweed. Finches and sparrows cheeped in the hedges. The going was slow. Eva saw no sign of human habitation for miles.

As the angle of the light changed, the backlit weeds shone and waved like shabby royalty in the evening breeze. Eva tried to enjoy the simple pleasure of being on a horse, free to go where she chose, but her nerves twitched. When a bright orange fox leapt above the tall grass, Eva inhaled sharply and paused. After that she kept her eyes trained on the ground, looking for anything that might turn out to be dinner.

She was about to break down and open the bag of nuts she'd bought for emergency rations when she glanced up and saw that the road stopped abruptly in front of her. A dense stand of trees towered overhead. Their trunks were too big for a new forest. Yet they pushed up right through the pavement, close-ranked as soldiers in formation. She could see no way through. She gazed to the right, then to the left, trying to get a sense of the extent of the forest.

She got down off the horse and walked, looking for some way in and through. Slowly she paced along the edge of the trees, leading the horse. Between the trunks—narrow gaps no wider than a good book—she saw no light, no glimmer of distant space. Eventually she stopped and stared at the trees. There was something odd and yet familiar about them.

Eva glanced up at the sky, which had taken on the violet cast that precedes evening. She wondered if she should settle in for the night and try to find a way around in the morning. She sighed and leaned a hand on one of the massive trunks. The bark tingled against her palm. She pulled her hand away and examined it, hoping there weren't some sort of tiny thorns. She took a closer look at the tree, trying to identify it by its leaves. This time there seemed to be more space between the tree and the one next to it. Puzzled, she stepped closer. The tangled thorny undergrowth at her feet bent and bowed as if a door had opened into the woods. She peered ahead. Where a moment before the forest had appeared impenetrable, now she could discern a narrow gap extending through the trees.

She looked back at the darkening sky and listened hard, trying to gauge the nature of the woods. A rabbit darted across the path in front of her and disappeared. A moment later an owl swooped close and flew off without a sound.

She began to walk slowly through the woods, following the path that seemed to open as she approached.

After a few minutes she stopped and looked back, and was somehow not surprised to see the path behind her had vanished. The path ahead remained. Carefully, but with a growing feeling of confidence, she continued, leading the calm horse, until after perhaps fifteen minutes, or it could have been a seamless hour, they came to a small mossy glade. Darkness enveloped them, but Eva found she could see, even though there was no clear view of the sky. The tree canopy was so dense and quiet Eva almost felt as if she were underground. She tied the horse to a tree and took off its saddle. She pulled out the last two apples from her pack, gave one to the horse, and sat down on a rock to eat the other as slowly as she could.

She woke from a deep, dreamless sleep and sat up quickly, her heart pounding. The quiet of the night had given way to the rustle and murmur of distant birdsong and movement in the branches overhead. As she sat up she noticed a small pile of berries and nuts arranged on a leaf the size of a plate. She was ravenous, but she wondered who or what had left the food for her. After a few moments her hunger persuaded her to have faith in the forest. It had let her in, she reasoned. If it were a trap, it could have killed her easily enough while she slept. She looked up into the cloaking canopy and murmured, "Thank you." Then she ate everything.

Refreshed, she untied the horse, who appeared to have found a patch of grass to eat. Trying to decide which way to go, Eva looked around the glade, disoriented by the lack of sunlight. She shrugged and took a step toward the tree line. Again a gap widened at her approach. She bowed slightly, acknowledging the welcome, and stepped further into the forest.

As before, the path opened in response to her. She began to feel at ease, accepting that, whatever this place was, its intentions toward her seemed benevolent. As the day wore on, each time she stopped to rest she found more provisions laid out for her. When her thirst grew uncomfortable the path led her to a small clear stream rushing over a rocky bed. She drank her fill and continued on. The forest seemed to go on forever.

Toward the end of the second day she tripped over a moss-covered brick. She stooped to take a closer look. She felt along the moss and found other bricks. Creeping slowly in the direction of the bricks, she came upon a tree surrounding a door. The door wasn't in the tree. The tree looked as if it had grown right up through the sill. As Eva peered around the tree, she spied a glint of glass, almost obscured by vines. She took a step back and realized that an entire wall of a house was interwoven with tree trunks and branches. She was trying to find a way around the remnants of wall when she noticed a gate, nearly covered with vines. She pushed against it gently, expecting it to be rotten, but it swung open easily, revealing an open space, a town square of sorts. Mossy cobblestones floored the clearing. Ancient-looking board-and-batten buildings leaned in as if to whisper secrets to each other.

There was no light in the windows, no smoke from the chimneys, not a whisper save for the murmur of the leaves above. As Eva's eyes grew accustomed to the half-light filtering in from the forest, she noticed a mossy water trough in the center of the space. She led the horse to it. While the horse drank, a raccoon waddled out from one of the buildings and stood on its hind legs, checking her out.

"Hi," Eva said.

The raccoon appeared to raise an eyebrow, but preserved its silence, and waddled off slowly.

"Okay then," Eva said to the trees. "I guess this is as good a place as any to spend the night."

She poked around a bit inside the abandoned buildings and found birds' nests, colonies of mice and plenty of rabbit droppings, but nothing of value. Eventually she curled up under the eave of what might have been a tavern once upon a time, but it took her a while to fall asleep. She kept wondering what had happened to all the people who must have lived here once, and if anyone at all was left in upstate New York. A small black cat slipped in beside her and curled up, purring. Eva drifted off to sleep.

She woke slowly, smiling sleepily at the sight of the cat still at her side. Then she caught sight of something else and sat up fast.

An older woman with silver hair and deep lines in a face that still held beauty was watching her with an expression of mild curiosity. "Good morning," she said, in a low, musical voice.

Eva stared at the woman, noticing her dress of intricately woven leaves and grasses. Her feet were shod in delicate slippers of russet grass.

"Hello," Eva said. "Who are you?"

The woman studied Eva for a moment. "You don't need to know my name, Eva."

"How do you know mine?"

"You weren't exactly low-profile around these parts. You tore up a lot of good work when you fashioned that fancy castle."

Eva's eyes widened. "You know about that?"

"What I don't know is why you've come back. The whisper in the wind said the Mother had drowned you when She washed out the taint of Deep Magic. Yet here you are. Why?"

"Wait. Does everyone think I'm dead?"

"I can't say for everyone, but we of the Thicket thought we'd seen the last of you. And we weren't sorry." She held Eva's eyes with a long look. "Have you changed?"

"Yes. I have. I didn't understand a lot of things. But now... I've learned a little."

The woman didn't smile, but a softer light came into her eyes. "Well. I guess we'll see. The Thicket accepted you. That's something."

"What is the thicket?"

The woman held her arms out in a gesture that took in the forest surrounding them. "All of this," said the woman.

Eva glanced around at the abandoned village. "You mean this town?"

The woman shook her head. "The town had nothing to do with this place. The Thicket has reclaimed it."

"So... This thicket is fast growing, huh?"

The woman raised an eyebrow and gave Eva a long look.

"I mean," Eva continued hurriedly, "when I came in... When I touched one of the trees... I felt..." She paused, eyeing the woman carefully.

"You felt the magic."

"Yes. I thought it was all gone."

"Most of it is. But even the Mother wouldn't destroy the rootstock of all that is magical. The cleansing floods washed the seeds far from the grasp of mankind. The spirit of the miraculous has returned to its ancient hiding places. This place, and all such, are designed to repel the inquisitive invasions of humans. Yet it allowed you to enter. I'd like to know why."

Eva frowned. "Well, I don't get it. I've lost my magic. I can't do anything anymore. I couldn't even conjure a hotdog when I was starving."

The woman gazed at her thoughtfully. "Yet the Thicket opened itself to you."

"So?"

"So there must be more to you than is apparent."

"Huh. Speaking of parents, I really need to make things right with mine. Am I going to be able to get out of here anytime soon, do you think? I mean, this is interesting and all, but, really, I'm in kind of a hurry because...well, there's some people I need to see."

The woman pursed her lips and looked long at Eva before she said, "Perhaps."

"What do you mean, 'perhaps'?"

"Perhaps the reason you are here, where no other human has been permitted since the Greening took root, is that your destiny is somehow part of the tapestry."

"The what?"

"The great tapestry, the infinite interconnected pattern of life in this corner of the universe. Every world is founded on some fundamental source—an unquenchable fire, a perpetual spring, an endless song. Earth's great power flows from the life force of its trees. Without these, this world dies."

"Are you saying that the trees are the source of all magic?"

"Magic exists in the trees. But the trees are more important than magic. Mankind will not survive without trees."

Eva frowned in thought. After a few minutes she said, "So what has this got to do with me?"

The woman laughed softly. "That is the question." She sighed and stood up. "We cannot always understand The Mother's plan. But it's clear that you are part of it."

Eva shrugged. "So what now? Am I supposed to wait here for a sign? Or can I go?"

The woman inclined her head with a slight smile. "You are free to go. If you can."

Eva stood up. "Okay then. I'm leaving. Maybe." She looked at the woods surrounding them and took a few steps closer.

As Eva stared at the impenetrable forest, one of the trees shimmered almost imperceptibly, and a narrow gap widened, leading into the dark woods.

"I guess that's my path," Eva said, turning to take a last look at the woman, who was watching her intently. "I know we may never meet again, but just out of curiosity, would you tell me your name now? Since I'm part of the tapestry and all?"

The woman's lips curved into something like a smile. "I am the Weaver. That's all the name you need from me."

"Huh. Okay. It was nice meeting you."

And with that, Eva stepped into the Thicket and vanished from sight.

CHAPTER 23

Peach-colored clouds drifted high above the wide river. Clayton sat near the cliff's edge, tuning his guitar and watching the sunset's glow fade in the river's reflection. Mudley sat beside him, head up, sniffing scents on the rising breeze. Once or twice the dog looked up at Clayton expectantly before turning his gaze back to the river.

Clayton gave a small sigh and began to play his sunset song. Mudley settled down and rested his head on his paws as the music began. The clear, simple melody took wing on the evening air and flew across the river as it did each night. Clayton didn't sing the words, though they were written on his heart.

For six months he and Mudley had kept watch over the site where Eva's castle had melted into sand during the first days of the Rain. While all the other people who had worked for Eva fled, Clayton hunkered down. He fashioned a crude hut out of salvaged boards and tree limbs that washed up on the river's shore. He scavenged a genuine Turkish rug and a priceless Belgian tapestry from the castle ruin to insulate his shelter. He fished and trapped to feed himself and Mudley. It had been a long, cold winter.

Now the planet had begun its tilt toward the sun again, and Clayton carefully guarded the pilot light of hope that kept his campfire burning. Even after he learned the extent of the Rain, while rumor mills and gossip vines crackled with accounts of doom and death, he held fast to his faith in Eva. She would return. She had to.

As the first star winked into light, Mudley sat up quickly, his eyes shining, his nose quivering. Clayton stilled his fingers and listened to the night air. Sometimes vandals and thieves came around the cliffs, looking for anything left worth stealing. Clayton reached for the knife strapped to his boot and stood up quietly.

At first he could hear nothing but the distant murmur of the river and the rustle of spring leaves. Then, at the edge of the darkness he heard it—the rhythm of steps, coming closer. The tread was slow, but not stealthy. And more than two feet, by the sound of it. Clayton frowned. He was brave, but not foolish. One man with a knife wasn't a sure bet against two or three men with fists.

But Mudley was bouncing on his paws, wagging his tail. Suddenly, to Clayton's dismay, the little dog let loose a piercing howl that startled the birds out of the nearby trees.

"Shhh!" Clayton hissed. In the instant of silence that followed he noticed the sound of footsteps had stopped. His heart was pounding as he gripped the knife closer to his chest.

"Mudley? Is that you?"

Her voice sent chills running down his thighs and up his arms. She pulled her horse to a stop at the edge of the woods and stared at Clayton. He gaped at her, his mouth open. Like a man in a dream he lowered the knife, unhooked the guitar from its strap and set it down on the ground.

"You're here," she said in a tone of gentle disbelief.

"I never left," he said.

"I'm not the same," she said hurriedly, climbing down off the horse. "I don't have any magic anymore."

"Yes, you do," he said.

She stepped closer. In her face he saw the girl he had loved, and someone else. The look in her eyes no longer had the sharp challenge that masked her defensive edge. Her gaze was clear and open. Her eyes met his with warmth and gratitude.

"How did you..." he began.

"It's a long story. I'll tell you all about it. But...I don't really want to talk now."

Mudley bounded to her, wriggling with joy. She knelt and hugged him. "Mudley, you silly dog. I missed you." She looked up into Clayton's eyes and smiled.

He came to her then and pulled her to her feet. He looked deep into her eyes and took her in his arms and held her while his heart raced.

After a moment she pulled back and said, "I'm so sorry. For everything. You know that, right?"

He nodded.

"I guess there's nothing left here? I mean, the Rain..." she faltered.

He shook his head.

She sighed, enjoying the feeling of being cradled in his arms. He didn't seem in any hurry to talk or to let her go. She bit her lip and said, "I guess there's no reason for me to stay here."

Clayton raised his eyebrows.

"I mean," she went on hurriedly, "Except for you, of course. But... I have to straighten some things out with my family."

He tilted his head, the expression in his eyes quizzical.

"I mean, I really need to talk to my mom and I don't even know where she is. And I want to find my dad and make things right with him and—"

Clayton put a gentle finger on her lips. "You can do all of that," he said. "But first, I think you owe Mudley an apology. Because, you know, he's been waiting patiently for like, six months, and it hasn't been easy for him and—"

Then she stood on her toes and pressed her lips against his and surrendered herself to a moment of purest joy. More magical than any spell, more thrilling than any adventure.

***

The next morning, after they'd scrounged something to eat and fed Mudley and the horse, whom Clayton insisted on naming Charles, they began the long walk to D.C., the first stop on what Eva was calling her Reconciliation Tour.

"I've got to make things right with my mom. And Josh. And I think I didn't give my dad a chance either."

"You should definitely do that," Clayton said, as he loaded his few possessions onto Charles's back. "Not everybody gets to have a father, you know."

Eva nodded. "Yeah. I've been a jerk." She gazed across the river and frowned. "That seems like a lot of smoke for this time of day."

Clayton narrowed his eyes and looked across the river. "Yeah. Some people say the fires are started by lightning. But we haven't had any this spring."

"Huh. Strange."

"Yeah."

"I guess there's no one to fight fires anymore."

"Not so much."

"Maybe it'll burn itself out."

Clayton stared at the towering smoke plume drifting above the distant treeline. "Maybe."

***

Henry Auldridge watched the dark smoke billow higher, blotting out the sun, and grinned like a child smashing a piñata.

Henry had spent nineteen years inside a tree.

Most of those years he boiled with rage. A few of them he endured in a cold frozen sulk. But as the years went by his wrath grew sharper, more pointed. He didn't know if he'd ever get the chance to put his dream of revenge into action, but if that day ever dawned, he wouldn't have to waste time planning.

When the Rain began pelting the great forest in upstate New York where Henry lurked under the bark of a majestic oak, he didn't take much notice at first. Rain, snow, wind, heat, what did he care?

But as the constant rain continued day after day, Henry began to sense something different, almost like movement in his veins. This was unusual. Ever since his physical body had been grafted to the tree he had had difficulty separating his own sensations from the tree's. Now, while he sensed the tree's response to the insistent deluge, Henry experienced a thrilling tingle in what had once been his very own arms and legs. A gentle thudding in his chest grew stronger with each day. Henry felt a surge of warmth as his magic-tainted blood gave way to hot, red juice flowing through his veins.

And when, after a wet week, his eyes, shuttered for so long, blinked open and he found that he could see through the membrane of cells still holding him inside the tree, Henry's fury flamed hotter as he writhed to break free.

But his human body was weak. So weak. His muscles hadn't flexed in so long. His frustration mounted like steam in a piston but he could do nothing. Yet he was so close now, so close.

He watched the rain streaming down and realized with a clarity that calmed him that the membrane enclosing him was slowly vanishing. With each passing hour his vision was getting clearer, as if the rain were dissolving the magical bonds that had tormented him for so long. All he had to do was wait. He gritted his teeth, smiling grimly to himself as he felt the movement of his tongue exploring the wet wall of his mouth. Soon, he told himself, soon he would be released.

He didn't know how or if he would be able to find the tree-huggers who had ruined his life, but he didn't need to find them to execute his plan. Those eco-freaks thought they'd gotten rid of Henry. But they'd find out just how wrong they were.

They'd had their fun. Now there would be hell to pay.

The End

Book Two of The Greening

About the Author

Constance Sprague was born in Erie, PA, a quiet under-the-radar city with no illusions about itself. She continues to saunter to the beat of a different drummer in the Washington, D.C., area, where she remains a closet whistler, a lifelong daydreamer, and a competent roller skater. She is the author of a half dozen novels, most of them bearing little relation to reality.

Find news and information about her current and upcoming projects at http://www.constancesprague.com.